I0629397

An Appalachian Nightmare

Cole William Barnhill

The story, all names, characters, and incidents portrayed in this production are fictitious. No identification with actual persons (living or deceased), places, buildings, and products is intended or should be inferred.

The author acknowledges the trademark status and trademark owners of various products referenced in this work. The publication/use of these trademarks is not associated with or sponsored by the trademark owners.

AN APPALACHIAN NIGHTMARE Copyright© 2024 by Cole William Barnhill. All rights reserved.

Cover Art by Cole William Barnhill

ISBN: 979-8-218-47775-2

First Edition: 2024

For my family,

the ones I was born with

and the ones I've made along the way.

hear them cry
the long dead
the long gone
speak to us
from beyond the grave
guide us
that we may learn
all the ways
to hold tender this land
          bell hooks, Appalachian Elegy

One

I had just turned sixteen the first time I went to a funeral and understood it. I had been to funerals before. Everyone had. Death in Appalachia was a constant. Still is, I guess. But before that one, none of them had ever hit me in the same way as they seemed to hit other people.

Before then, they had just been an event I had to go to and get through. I didn't really care, though. Death wasn't a big deal to me—it was just something that all of us had to do eventually.

The funeral was for Mom's best friend, Marianne. I knew her okay, but I wouldn't say we were close. I would go with Mom to visit with her sometimes. I'd sit on the couch and try to be polite. I'd listen if they talked about something interesting, but most of the time it was just gossip about other people in the town that I didn't really care about.

I had never cared about the drama in Bellwether. A lot of people did. Mom did. Marianne did. Bellwether gossip just made me sad for everyone who lived there, not just the people who had been done wrong. The people who were doing the wrong normally had a reason. Their lives always seemed to be pretty bad.

Marianne had always been into drugs. *It was the seventies. Everyone did LSD*, she had said. She lost herself in powder and pills in the nineties. It was the natural progression for an addict, I guess. She never had any interest in getting clean, and Mom never tried to stop her. Mom never let me see that Marianne had a problem. I didn't know until later, and I had to learn it from other people.

In '04 the coke wasn't clean, and God knows what got in it. Mom found her. I was at school, but folks said you could hear the screams across town. I don't know about that, but Mom didn't seem to stop wailing until the funeral. It was a sight to see. My father wasn't kind about it, but he went to the funeral. *It's what husbands do*, he'd said.

I had never seen Mom so emotional, but seeing her at that funeral, watching her tear in half as they lowered Marianne into the ground—it was obvious Marianne's death absolutely undid her. I know my father caused her own eventual death, but Marianne's dying certainly didn't help.

I wore a black dress to the funeral. I almost never wore dresses. Mom made me. It was just the proper way people dressed for funerals. I felt uncomfortable the entire time. Mom thanked me. That made it worth it.

After the service, Mom stood with Marianne's family in the receiving line. People kept giving me their condolences and telling me how brave I was for not crying. I wasn't being brave; I just didn't care.

I shook hands and faked my smile and thanked the nice people for being nice and saying the nice things. Mom was still crying, but her voice had gone. Maybe she started dying when the wailing stopped—the gun just ended the process.

Halfway through the hugs and attempts at sympathetic looks, I started crying. I wasn't sure why. I didn't think I was sad. I hadn't known Marianne that well. But Mom was crying, and I loved my mom. I loved being her daughter, and she loved being Marianne's friend. So Mom's grief became mine.

When my face was wet and my cheeks were red, Mom turned and gave me a hug. There wasn't a break in the line, she just turned from them and gave me a hug.

"I love you," she said.

I wish I could have the memory tattooed into my brain. She held my hand by the outside of my palm and squeezed it for comfort.

Mom and I rode back to the house with my father after the funeral was over. It was cold out. The grief had taken all of the warmth out of the year—all of the good.

* * *

It was colder after Mom died. It snowed for days. I thought it would never end. The ground was frozen solid.

God didn't want her yet. I wanted him to let her come home. Maybe that's why I didn't really believe in God.

I was seventeen then.

* * *

It was hot when my father died. It was spring, and it was in the middle of an almighty heat wave. Hell wanted him and Beelzebub was waiting.

We were learning about Shakespeare in school at the time. My best friend, Katie, pointed out a line to me: "more light than heat." She told me that was my father.

I agreed. I was eighteen.

* * *

I wished I got to go to my ex-husband's funeral. That is, I wished he were dead. He was a son of a bitch and never treated me all too well, but he was my husband and losing that sort of constant presence still hurts. It has to hurt, there's no way to avoid it.

It wasn't a surprise when Jeff left. I knew he was hunting for jobs out of town, and I knew we had been talking less. I came home one day, and he was packing his things. I understood. There was no big argument. It just was what it was; there was nothing more to talk about. Our marriage, such as it was, was no longer.

He left for good late one evening, right after we signed the last of our divorce papers and I put my ring in the drawer. I helped him put the last bag in his truck and didn't cry when he pulled away. I wished him well with his new job and exhaled a weight off my shoulders as I walked back inside. I felt lousy. I tried to act brave about it, but I needed a distraction. That meant the creature comforts of an old haunt.

Two

"My husband left," I told the bartender as he turned to me. I rapped my knuckles three times on the hardwood bar top so the sting would keep me from crying. I always thought it was just a trope, telling a bartender your woes, but there I was.

"Shoot. Seems to be a common thread around here—wife left last month," he responded, tossing a broken wine glass into the garbage. "Got a new job in the city and said she was done with this godforsaken town and its godforsaken people. Told me I'm one of 'em."

I just grimaced at him. I didn't think there was really anything to say, anyway. Breakups are hard. Divorces are harder. In that moment I would have preferred Jeff had murdered me instead of just leaving. There wasn't even another woman, he had just had enough. It was never a great marriage, but it was what I knew—and the undoing of what I knew stung me like a hornet. Sudden change is hard that way. I once heard it described as the arcane word *wuthering*—the sudden obliteration of future expectations.

"Care to share a drink?" The bartender placed both hands on the counter in front of me. He was still wearing his ring, but it looked more decorative than declarative. "On the house."

On cue, the bells on the front door chimed. It was only me, the lone bartender, and a couple of kids from the local high school who had really bad fake IDs. They didn't get served, but the as yet anonymous bartender let them stay to have some sodas. The kids seemed content with that outcome.

Oh, and Jack. That wasn't his real name, but I knew him as Jack. I think everyone only ever knew him as Jack, aside from his parents, I guess. He was a drug dealer who always sat in the corner. Everyone knew it; no one cared. He wasn't in the business of bothering people, and people weren't in the business of bothering him. He was almost like a movie stereotype come to life.

I heard the chime of the door opening and turned over my shoulder to see two people whom I didn't recognize. They clearly weren't locals, and taking in their appearance, I assumed they had never been to a proper small town before—much less in Appalachia. I doubted they even knew *how* to handle a town with one good grocery store and a main street which is actually the only main street.

The man had on brown loafers, jeans which had never been worn for yard work, a brown belt, white button-up shirt, and blue blazer. His jeans had an imprint from a cellphone in the front pocket and a sizable money clip in the back. The woman wore a blue seersucker dress and high heels. On her hand was a diamond ring the size of Kansas hail. I hated them both on sight.

I didn't know how they ended up in my hometown, and I didn't care. I hoped they wouldn't get served. There weren't many reasons people like them ever stepped foot in Bellwether, and none of them were good. They didn't belong and they knew it—they embraced it.

The woman had the implied motion and the same kind of hate as a looming cloud that's formed but hasn't yet decided whether it's going to rain. The man smiled at no one except his own ego and buttoned up that stupid blazer as he strutted to the barstool two down from mine.

Perhaps they wanted to see what poor really looks like. Maybe they were hoping I would be the next victim of the opioid epidemic right there in front of them—and maybe I was considering it, too. But I wasn't a junkie. I didn't do drugs. I had lost plenty of friends to them, though. Everyone had. That's the way it goes.

"I'll share a drink with you if you tell me your name." I turned my attention back to the bartender and smiled sarcastically.

I used to go to the bar a lot more. It was right down the street from my place and used to have a nice vibe that I liked. It was a small bar, maybe fifty seats, but homey. I still liked it, but Jeff didn't, so it had been a few years. Jeff was gone, so fuck him. I could do what I wanted, and I wanted to go get a drink. It had barely changed since the last time I came in. How much could it have changed, really? Nothing changes quickly around Bellwether. To show me the mild breadth of time that had passed, the barstools were all faded, but some of the tables were new— so was the bartender.

"Theodore." He reached out a hand to shake.

"The fuck kind of name is Theodore around here?" I shook his hand. I made sure to shake it firm, so he knew I wasn't an easy target. This seemed like a shtick, well practiced. Theodore wasn't getting laid that night. At least not by me.

"The one my mama gave me." He shot back quickly with a grin. It used to be that I knew all the bartenders in there, but I didn't know this guy. I liked his sass, though. "She saw it in the newspaper and liked it. Gave it to me. I've had it as long as I've lived."

"What Theodore did she see?" I asked, trying to think of a famous Theodore. "You're clearly named after someone real, no?"

"You don't want to know." Theodore grabbed two tumbler glasses and set them down in front of us.

"You're named after the fucking Unabomber, aren't you?" I laughed heartily at him. The blazer was staring at me, so I shot him a look and flexed my forearms. I have strong arms, and I wanted him to know it.

"No." He laughed. "How young do you think I am? I have no idea who my namesake is. Mama just liked the name is all."

"Fair enough," I conceded. "Still, that would've been pretty damn funny. Little Theodore, named for the Unabomber. Can't imagine you'd have ended up here."

That was Blazer and Blue Dress's cue to leave. We had sufficiently scared them. People in Bellwether tend to do that to outsiders. It ain't for everyone.

"Got a last name Theodore?" I ignored Blazer as he walked a little too close to me on the way out.

"I got one if you've got a name." He grinned. I could see how his charade was supposed to play out and decided to humor him a little longer.

"Jesse Strotherton." I reached out and shook his hand again.

"You were making fun of Theodore with a last name like that?" He smirked, accepting my handshake. "Townes. Theodore Townes is my full name."

"The Unabomber and the country singer. What a man."

"Funny enough, people in my family can't stand ol' Townes Van Zandt. If for no other reason than because it's the only thing people associate with our name." He chuckled and took a sip. "I like him, but I wouldn't ever admit it to my kin."

He threw a little extra drawl on the word *kin* so it held more punch than a single syllable. I shook my head and swirled my drink.

"That's funny," I said and downed the last of my whiskey. "Well, Theodore Townes. It's been a pleasure."

I set down my empty tumbler and stood up to walk out. You can bet I noticed him watching me the whole way to the door.

* * *

Not every day is as exciting as the night you get left by your husband. The next morning sure wasn't. My six o'clock alarm sure seemed rude, but I was the one who set it. The pathetic fallacy, my high school English teacher called it, giving human emotions to non-human things. My clock didn't mean to be rude; it was a hunk of wires.

That thing doesn't know or care that when I get up in the morning it's because I have to go to work. It doesn't know I don't want to do that, but I do it, anyway. I need money, at least that's what my landlord tells me.

I worked for the mayor. Before you go and think that's fancy or I was some kind of bigwig, hold your horses. Remember, this is a small town, and I was still poor. I would answer the phone and transcribe things into spreadsheets. Sometimes I got to escort visitors to his office, but most of the time, someone who was genuinely important did that.

I wasn't even allowed to do any kind of scheduling or make any decisions when I answered the phone—I just transferred the calls to the people who could. But I worked for the mayor, and that seemed like a fairly important thing.

Mayor Wright seemed to be a good man. I always felt like he tried to make the right decision. That's why I worked for him. Well, that and the fact that he gave me a job.

I mean, I disagreed with him on most things political, but he was also a hell of a lot smarter than me, based on the multiple diplomas on his wall. So I sort of tried to stick to my station and not cause problems. My best value was my ability to show up, get my work done, and not be noticed most of the time.

Not to mention, he hadn't made a decision that had really screwed me yet. Not that I was aware of, at least.

He always treated me fairly, gave me time off when I needed it. He paid me enough to live on in Bellwether, and I didn't need any more than that. He didn't necessarily know a whole lot about my life, but he didn't need to. He didn't ask me about my family, and I'm glad he didn't because then I would have to tell him about my family.

One of the things I did like about Bellwether is that you don't have to look too nice to do a job. Mayor Wright looked like a typical mountain hick from Bellwether. He was six-two and had a crooked, toothy smile. His beard was relatively well trimmed, all things considered, but it was speckled gray to show his age, and his hair wasn't exactly Hollywood. He dressed decently enough, but I never saw him wear a suit, and I never saw him without cowboy boots and his belt buckle.

I actually liked the belt buckle. Not really my style, but it was pretty classy. It was silver with an etching of a cardinal. If your mayor is going to wear a belt buckle, you'd want it to be this one. As long as you live in a state where the state bird is a cardinal. Maybe he would wear a different belt buckle if he lived in Tennessee, I don't know.

The day after my husband left, Mayor Wright came into the office a little later than usual. He always got in early, that's why I also had to get up so damn early in the morning. That's why nine o'clock seemed real late for him to be getting to the office. He never came in at a time that a normal worker would be coming in, he worked too hard for that.

I didn't mind, though. It gave me time to rev up for the day and to steel my face. I had three coffees before Mayor Wright walked in the door that morning. I normally had one. My hands were shaking like leaves. I looked like an alcoholic drying out. I felt about as bad as I imagine that feels.

"Sorry I'm late," Mayor Wright said softly when he finally game in. He stopped in front of my desk. He never stopped in front of my desk. "Senator Blythe died last night. Heart attack. Never even made it to the hospital."

Senator Roosevelt Blythe was the state senator who represented Bellwether in addition to a few other small towns. He was, no joke, 103 years old when he died. I'm fairly certain he voted against the Thirteenth Amendment. He made a career on being old and racist. It's entirely possible that he had born fifty years old.

He won his first election for this same seat when he was only thirty-seven. He served the majority of thirty-three terms. *Thirty-three.*

I never wanted to hold a job for that long. To be fair, I didn't want to live to be 103, either. That's just too much life. Living is nice and all, but I was thirty-one at that point and was already really tired. Seventy-two more years seemed like just too much. There has to be a lot of heartbreak in a timespan like that. A lot of family come and gone—far too many funerals attended.

The poor old bastard's wife had died forty years prior, and every one of his six kids had died in the time since then. Apparently, he had grandkids. They didn't live here anymore. I can't imagine they ever came to visit their grandad; they had all left for a reason. Maybe they had visited when he was at the state capital. That's a nice thought. Probably not, though.

"I'm sorry to hear that, sir. He was a good man," I lied, thinking maybe this morning wouldn't be so boring, after all.

"Yeah, well . . ." Mayor Wright seemed to debate whether or not he should tell the truth. "It's a big loss in the state. I woke up to a call from the governor; that's why I'm late. Governor Wyche is coming to town later. He's going to give a speech, it sounds like. Wants me to talk—say some nice things about Senator Blythe. Guess that's what I'm doing today now. You can forward any calls about him to Jeffrey."

Jeffrey Plum was the communications director/press secretary for Mayor Wright. I didn't like him. Thin guy, hollow cheeks, and slick black hair. Real ambitious right-wing type guy. Always wore a black suit. Made Mayor Wright look underdressed. Dress for the job you want, I guess. I hoped Jeffrey would never get the job he wanted. But I was glad he had to answer questions about Senator Blythe and not me.

"Did you hear that the governor is coming later?" I heard a whisper behind me.

"Yes actually, Mayor Wright told me." I swung around and smiled at Bill Westfield.

Bill was the custodian at city hall. He had been around for almost as long as Senator Blythe, except for Bill was actually a great man. At one time he was all of six feet tall and a brave soldier in Vietnam. Even though he hadn't agreed with the war, he went because he knew what he had signed up for. I loved that about Bill. In his old age he was maybe five-ten and always wore the same blue jeans and faded baseball cap.

It was not an exaggeration to say Bill was the nicest person in city hall. He didn't have an agenda, he just wanted to put in a day's work—as he had his entire life. His wife was the typical stay-at-home mom of the seventies. She was still alive, and he still loved her with all he had. I had met her one time—sweet lady, too. Their kids were the rare breed who actually came back to visit fairly regularly.

That says something about the Westfields. They were just damn good folks. I would've voted for Bill for mayor if I could. He'd never want it, though. It's always the best people who never go for it.

"Exciting times, dear." Bill grinned. His grin, more of a smirk, was deeply ingrained in his face from years of doing it. "Sad circumstances, of course," he almost whispered.

"Yes, sir, they really are." I tried to shift my tone.

Bill chuckled. "Surprised the old bastard lived this long—I was getting worried he'd outlive me." Bill laughed at his own joke and patted me on the arm. I loved that man, even in making a jab at an awful human, he still found a way to be humble and self-deprecating. "Got time for a coffee?"

Bill loved sitting and drinking a coffee with whomever would sit and chat. I really didn't have the time, but I always made it for Bill.

"For you"—I beamed—"of course I do!"

Three

"Bill?" I set down my coffee mug. It was too hot. I burned my mouth. Seems to me that's the only way to drink coffee. "How did you know that Cathy-Anne was the one?"

"Oh dear . . ." he sat back and smiled. I could see it in his eyes that he had gone back in time. "I just knew, the first time I ever talked to her."

Bill met Cathy-Anne Smith when he was twenty-three years old—right after he got back from Vietnam. He knew the war was lost and worried he would drink away his pain and lose the PTSD in the bottle, so his sister paid for him to go down to Florida for a couple of weeks. Put his toes in the sand and smell the salt water. Most importantly, try to forget about the war.

Cathy-Anne was working at his hotel, answering the phone, sort of like me. He wouldn't leave Florida without her. She wouldn't leave without a ring. He bought the nicest ring he could at a pawn shop in Boca Raton and brought home his bride-to-be to begin a new life. A life without war. A life of love and dedication and appreciation for the little things—like midday coffee and quality conversations.

"Yeah." I smiled. I wasn't happy in my own mind, but I was happy at Bill's love and joy. "I suppose we never did feel that."

"And that's okay, dear." Bill didn't let me finish the thought. For the best. "You're barely over thirty years old, for gosh sakes! You'll meet the one, and when you do, you won't be sitting here asking an old fart how to know, that's for darn sure."

"Thanks, Bill. I appreciate it."

* * *

My parents weren't the best role models when it came to love. First Lieutenant James K. Strotherton was born in Bellwether. He left once, to fight in Vietnam. He was proud of the war. I call it American exceptionalism; he thought it was America being exceptional. He told me about all of the men he had killed, how they were all filthy and worthless. I wondered if they thought that of him. I imagined they would've taken him out all the same if they could. If they had been given the chance, maybe they would have taken the shot, too. Sometimes I wished they had.

If you haven't noticed, just about everyone in Bellwether joined a branch of the military when they hit eighteen. No one went to college; everyone went off to die. *Better to die quickly at the end of an enemy gun than to rot away slowly in a factory in Ohio*, my father once told me. I never

19

believed him that those were the only two options. They weren't.

My father, the "war hero," met Carline Quincey when he got back from "the 'Nam." His parents knew her parents. She never had a choice. She would've killed him dead, too, if she'd had the chance.

She came from the family of *women are the weak and must be cared for by the big, strong man.* I never saw my mom speak up for herself. She never had a job. Never struck out on her own.

I guess that's why I was always such a rebel. My father hated how much of an attitude I had and how strong my opinions were. I got my fair share of beatings because of it. A double-pronged, silver studded, black leather belt was his weapon of choice. It hurt like a bitch, but I never cried. I never wanted him to think that he really hurt me. I never wanted him to know that I cared—never wanted to give him that sadistic satisfaction.

Mom died when I was seventeen. She swallowed the business end of a double-barreled shotgun. She wanted to know what lead tasted like. For her, it tasted like relief. I loved her, and I felt a weight taken off my shoulders when she went home to God. I left home soon after and went to work at the local Motel 6. That's where I learned to answer phones—it became my career, I guess. At least, I still do it.

My father died not long after I left. He finally found the bottom of a whiskey bottle and tried to pick a fight with someone who wasn't the size of a prepubescent girl. He ended up in a ditch, the man ended up in prison. A win for everyone involved, I think.

Maybe he loved Mom, and that's why he drank. But, really, I think he was just a drunk and a belligerent. He wanted to be The Man, but the Lieutenant did not always get his way.

I hated my father. Mom hated him more.

* * *

"Governor Wyche will be here in twenty minutes. Do you mind having a coffee ready for him? I'm sure he's had quite a long day," Christina Klein asked me when I got back into the office from my break with Bill.

Christina was Mayor Wright's executive secretary. Christina was great at her job. She went to college for it and everything. But she was also a sweet thing. All of sixty years old and five-foot-one, Christina had been around the block a couple times and knew exactly what she was doing—but she never made me feel bad when I didn't. She was everything you could want in a professional secretary.

If the President of the United States called with a request she didn't like, Christina could probably tell him off in a way that made him think she was doing him a favor. She could probably get the pope to change the opinion of the church without feeling like he was being worked. She could tell you your dog had been run over without making you cry.

Christina was fierce, she was tender, she was witty, and she was humble.

"Yes, ma'am, I can."

"He may not take it, but if we don't offer it, he probably is going to want it, and that's when we look bad." She dropped me a nugget of knowledge about the job without making me feel like she was.

I should probably explain. I live in Bellwether, Virginia.

Bellwether was supposedly named that way because in the 1920s, when the town was founded, some state politician who happened to be from the town thought it was the spitting image of a sage decider. It turns out the politician was wrong. Bellwether is redder than the blood drawn by its former residents for the cause of segregation. If Genghis Khan ran for office in Bellwether, he might be too liberal. Bellwether is many things, but it is certainly not a bellwether.

Though, if you ask me, Bellwether really isn't all that political these days. It might just be because I'm the lone liberal in town. Not that I'm even all that political. I just agree more with the liberals. I don't tell anyone that. It wouldn't be too prudent to say that I disagree with everyone I know.

Still, I'm not wrong. Folks don't talk about politics in Bellwether. Mostly they talk about the heat in the summer, and the rain—and sometimes snow—in the winter. It sometimes feels like there are only two types of weather we get here. Hell or Atlantis. Why pick one, when you can live in both at once?

I was born in Bellwether. I wouldn't say I hate my hometown, but I also wouldn't say I love it. Everything I have ever known and loved is here, but the things I love also tend to leave.

That's sort of the problem with Bellwether. It's a town that's just too big to really know anyone if you weren't born here but is just too small to have anything interesting. If someone happens to come into town, they leave just as quickly as they can. If someone is born here and is smart enough—and has enough money—they get out as fast as they can.

I knew Governor Wyche was entering city hall long before I ever saw a soul. His crew did not enter buildings quietly. They ran thirty deep, and the governor was toward the back of the pack, busily answering questions and walking where the herd lead him. He was, to my eye, *looking* important more than he was actually *doing* things that were important. The conversation overheard was more about scheduling than actual executive decision-making.

I don't know if he even saw me when he walked into the office. The first five or six people—I have no idea who they were or what they did, none of them introduced themselves to me—all asked me the same question. It wasn't actually a question, really, just a demand: "Let Mayor Wright know we're here."

Not that I had to, anyway. They were more than noisy enough to alert everyone else, too. Christina came out of the door between my desk and Mayor Wright's office to greet them—I sat in a lobby, basically, an antechamber before the actual office, but I didn't mind.

"Gentlemen how are we?" She smiled and disarmed the entire room, which went quiet. "Mayor Wright will be with you in just a moment, can Jesse and I get you all some coffees?"

A few of them said yes, including Governor Wyche, apparently. I still hadn't seen him yet, but according to one of his people, who not so politely directed me, he wanted six creams and four sugars in his coffee. It may just be me, but that ain't coffee. In my opinion, if you don't like black coffee, you don't actually like coffee. Governor Wyche liked milk and sugar, but Governor Wyche certainly didn't care about my opinion, so I didn't offer it.

Christina and I went into the office's little kitchen to prepare the coffee. Normally we have paper cups in addition to the mugs for everyone who works there—a benefit of working there was indeed getting to have your own personal mug of your choosing. Mine was a yellow smiley face mug like you might see on nineties' TV—nostalgia, I guess.

An early sign that a visit from the governor was a little more important than a normal visitor to city hall was that Christina had already laid out porcelain cups and sterling silver trays to carry the coffees on. I would never have thought to do that—Christina was damn good.

By the time we had all of the coffees ready, the group had been greeted by Mayor Wright and moved to the conference room. I had never been a waitress before. I cannot recommend it. Maybe it was the task of serving a bunch of men who made more in a week than I did in a month, but trying to get them to pay attention to me enough to simply hand them a coffee mug was a task and a half.

Christina was much more successful. She had a presence like that. She managed to set the tray of cream and sugars, as well as a tray of doughnuts that I'm pretty sure she manifested from nowhere, in the middle of the long wooden table without disturbing any of the men in suits.

After bringing in the coffee I followed Christina's lead and found a place against the wall by the door of the conference room. I understood our assignment—we were there in case any of the important people needed anything.

Christina was dedicated to that service to a greater good, but I didn't really care. I was there because it was a decent job, and I admit I wasn't much qualified for anything else.

"The weather seems to be good, so I would think that we ought to still be a go for our original plan." A lanky man with mousy brown hair started the meeting. I would later learn him to be the governor's chief of staff. I think his name was Nick. "We'll do a joint press conference/celebration of life at the gazebo in Blythe Park. Seems fitting to do it in the place named after him."

"I agree." Mayor Wright chimed in. "No objections over here."

"Good," Nick continued. "We'll have Mayor Wright speak first then introduce Governor Wyche. Mr. Mayor, we'll prepare remarks for you, so we can all be on the same page with our message."

"Nuh-uh. Not gonna do that, friend." Mayor Wright spoke up. I had never heard him put on the tough voice he was using now. "I will write my own remarks and deliver them how I want, and if not, we simply are not going to do this."

"Mr. Mayor—"

"Mayor Wright, you're a smart man. You know we have to do it this way," Governor Wyche told my boss sternly.

"And I know why you want to do it this way."

Mayor Wright stood.

Christina's face was steel. I couldn't tell what she was thinking. I know mine was betrayed by emotion.

"Okay, fine." The governor stood. "You can say what you want, but Nick"—it was Nick—"is going to give my introduction.

Mayor Wright nodded as the gang of gubernatorial staff stood up. Governor Wyche motioned for them all to leave.

"See y'all later," Mayor Wright said with a facetious tone.

It was a sunny but cool day at the park, the trees casting long shadows of chill on the ground. There was a crowd—not a big one but a crowd all the same—there to mourn their longtime state senator. I guess this was how he won elections, some folks had to have liked him.

The event went fine. All of that tussling in the meeting was just for show. Mayor Wright was kind—not glowing, but generous in his remarks. Nick gave a less-than-graceful introduction, and the governor spoke for way too damn long. Then everyone left the stage and went into the crowd to pretend to care. Mayor Wright did care—he just didn't like Senator Blythe. He was faking it, too, but in a different way.

The workday was done for me, but I felt like it wouldn't have been too classy for me to leave right after the speaking was done. I walked out into the crowd, trying

to stay near Mayor Wright in case he needed me—
Christina was there, so that wasn't too likely—but also
keep my distance.

I was walking through the crowd, trying to avoid
the folks I recognized and didn't want to talk to. That was
a lot of the folks in Bellwether, or at least the ones who
would come to a memorial for Senator Blythe on a
Thursday afternoon.

I was starting to feel like it was time for me to go
when I saw a familiar face standing a little bit away from
the crowd, just watching. One that I did want to talk to.

A tall string bean, tattoos peeking out from under
his shirt hiding unexpectedly muscular arms. A neat goatee
framing a crooked smile. Beaming eyes, the color of
electricity. You've never seen eyes so blue, I tell you that.

"If it ain't Jesse Strotherton herself." Theodore
could barely contain his grin.

"The very one." I curtsied and smiled back then
walked over to him. "What the hell are you doing at a thing
like this?"

"I should ask you the same damn question. Ain't
no way you like anyone here." The words rolled off his
tongue so easy and with a deep chuckle. "Curiosity, I guess.
I wanted to see if anyone would show up—see who I need
to not talk to anymore."

"Fair enough." I laughed. "I work for Mayor
Wright. I answer phones, sometimes put data in

spreadsheets. I'm about as damn low as you can rank to say you work for the mayor, if we're being honest."

Theodore looked over me into the crowd. He picked out Mayor Wright and observed him for a moment before looking back at me.

"Fair enough," he said. "He ain't a bad guy. You have to talk to the Gov today?"

"I was in the room but never talked to him." I told the truth.

"Fair enough again."

"So why aren't you at work?" I asked. I didn't want to sound like I was prodding too much.

"I don't go in 'til later this evening," he replied. "Bar doesn't really get goin' 'til nine or ten o'clock."

"Oh right." I felt stupid. I should've known bars work on different hours than the normal nine-to-five workweek.

"Think I'll be seeing you in there tonight?" His grin widened again.

"Oh, I don't know." I poked him in the arm. That was so awkward. *Why did I just poke him in the damn arm?* "Drinks free again tonight?"

"For pretty ladies." His crooked smile turned a little more sideways. He was proud of the joke he was about to make. "So you got to pay."

I chuckled.

"I'll see you around, Theodore." I shook my head and watched him as he walked away. His lanky frame gave him a funny sort of loping stride. It was oddly charming.

Four

I used to have a best friend in Bellwether, back before I became a loner divorcée. The kind of best friend who told me the truth about my father and knew all of the dark corners of my soul. I was younger back then, but Katie and I had been friends since we were real little. We went everywhere together. We were just about inseparable back in the day.

Part of the reason Bellwether was so safe for us back then was because everyone knew who we were. Not that folks in town didn't just generally know everyone else, but we were also pretty recognizable biking around town. Katie, what with her bright red hair. She always kept it in a ponytail, but even when she put it up it looked like a wildfire flame erupting from the back of her head.

We would fly around town, normally driven by some inane idea Katie had cooked up, just looking for trouble. We never got into real trouble— real danger, that is. We got fussed at plenty and got a few people's share of whoopings and groundings.

Once, in middle school, we decided we would egg our math teacher's house. Chucking as many eggs as you can at the home of someone you hate—or at least dislike—

may not be the best prank, but we were thirteen. You think stupid things are funny when you're thirteen.

Katie's parents had chickens back then. They would get so many eggs that they wouldn't always use them all. Normally the old rotten ones would get turned into feed, but we decided it would be funnier if we took some of the rotten ones to throw at Mr. Marino's house. I can't remember why we had a personal vendetta against Mr. Marino, but I'm not sure that it actually mattered.

It was Katie's job to steal the eggs, and my job to find the house. In a small town like Bellwether, it isn't that hard to figure out where people live—even for two school-age girls. We just sort of had to look around, pay attention.

We showed up with a basket of probably two dozen eggs, ready to let them rip. Not like the weak, super cleaned and sanitized white eggs you buy in the store. Natural, unwashed brown eggs from free-range chickens. They normally have thick shells.

I had the first throw. I picked up the top egg, spun it in my hand, and cocked back to let it fly. I threw forward with all my might but before it left my hand, the egg exploded on my fingers. Let me tell you, that thing *reeked*.

"What the heck?" I jabbed at Katie. "Your stupid chickens can't lay eggs with strong shells?!"

Katie let one rip and nailed a front window. It blew up in a flash of yellow filth.

"Strong enough to me." She turned to me and cocked her hip. "Maybe you're just throwing it wrong."

It was at that point that Mr. Marino walked out of the house next door.

"Hey, Mr. Marino," I said, not registering that we had just tagged some perfect stranger's home with a heinously rotten egg. "Wait—"

"Jesse?" He looked confused.

"You got the *wrong house*!!" Katie yelled at me.

"I was sure—"

Katie picked up another egg and let it fly at me. I turned to try and avoid it but ended up just getting hit right on the butt. It stung pretty bad, like a fat paintball. It smelled worse.

"You ass!" I cursed in front of a teacher.

I picked up an egg and returned the favor.

We pelted each other with those disgusting eggs until we were completely out of them—and absolutely covered in rotten, stinking goo. All the while, Mr. Marino was standing there taking in our bizarre situation.

"Time to bike on home, I think," he said, shaking his head when we were done and standing there covered egg. "We'll not discuss this Monday. I'll clear the air with my neighbors. Just get on out of here."

In hindsight, that was an incredibly generous response by him. He was a good man.

We had to go back to Katie's house and confront her parents with what we'd done. Oh my God, did we look a mess—and goddamn that smell. I'm sure we were a sight to see. Her dad hosed us off in the backyard. It was embarrassing—though, less embarrassing than egging the wrong house.

* * *

The bar was full when I walked in. I hadn't seen it full in years. Even before I had stopped going, it had been just about dead for a good while. I couldn't imagine a dramatic enough change to shift the business outlook that much during the intervening period.

In hindsight, it was a wonder the bar had stayed open at all. Rent was cheap in Bellwether, I guess. But still, rent is expensive when you don't have money to pay it. Maybe the building was grandfathered into some antiquated law. Perhaps it was actually a front for something else—not that I cared, anyway.

I hesitated by the door, not sure whether or not I actually wanted to go in. I wasn't sure if there was an event going on or something. It was noisy inside, certainly not sleepy enough to hear Theodore toss a broken glass quietly into a trash can full of mostly napkins and paper towels.

I realized after a visual sweep of the room that there was a small stage set up on the far end of the bar. Not so much a stage, really. More like a wood shipping pallet with a piece of plywood nailed on top. But the name of a stage is in the eye of the audience, I suppose.

Anyway, the stage wasn't what caught my eye, exactly. It was the string bean standing on the stage plucking away at an acoustic guitar. Theodore was a musician, apparently.

I snuck in, trying not to have him notice me, and found a seat at the bar on the end closest to the door, near to my usual spot. I was squeezed between two very different groups of people. One was trying hard to have a conversation; one was trying hard to listen to Theodore over the first group. Both seemed to hate the other—I simply found them humorous, if a bit annoying. I didn't recognize anyone in either group well enough to speak to them. They were most likely folks I had gone to high school with, but I had no interest in reliving those glory days with people I probably didn't even like at the time.

I wanted to be close to the door in case I decided to sneak out—Mom always taught me to have an exit strategy, no matter where you go. *Always park your car so that you can get out quickly if you need to*, she would say to me. I learned, whether it was the moral of her lesson or not, to be dubious of the world around me —she had me convinced it was going to kill me someday. Her logic wasn't far off, I suppose, as sad as it may be.

Apparently, I had come in near the end of the "show." Theodore played only two more songs—country tunes I vaguely recognized.

I say *songs* loosely. He was decidedly not good at what he was doing. His guitar playing was serviceable, at best, and his vocals left a world of training to be desired. But he was an employee at the bar, so maybe they were just being nice and letting him play. Low stakes, good karma. Good karma is hard to come by in a place like Bellwether.

I ordered a double bourbon on the rocks. Double because I needed to get a little intoxicated to get through the music—Theodore's slightly off-the-fret fingering was hard on the ears when he didn't find the chord quite right. Bourbon because it's good, sue me.

"So what did you think?" I could hear the smile on Theodore's voice. I hadn't seen him walk up in front of me—my ears were still ringing from the noise, so perhaps I wasn't quite on my game. Maybe the bourbon was kicking in.

"Don't quit your day job, bud." I tried to be charitable, but there wasn't much charity to be given. He smiled knowingly, and I couldn't help but snicker a little.

"Wasn't plannin' on it, my dear. Was not plannin' on it anytime soon," he said as he refilled my glass. He scratched his nose in a way that made me have half a mind to think he'd just done a bump in the bathroom, but I ignored the feeling and powered on. "They're nice to let me get up there, but to tell you the truth, I've heard cows getting slaughtered that sound better than I do up there singing. Don't say nothing about my guitar playing, though—my daddy taught me to play when I was a little fella, and in my own mind, I can goddamn shred."

I motioned zipping my lips and throwing away the key. He really—giving him as much grace and credit as I possibly could—was just not that good, though. But I decided to play nice.

Besides, his pronunciation of *gee-taur* described his accent pretty well, and I found it charming. I did wonder where the hell he might have heard cows getting slaughtered, though. There weren't really any farms near Bellwether. Plenty of folks had chickens. A couple up the hill had some goats, but that's about it. It could have just been a weird saying, I guess. If it was, it wasn't a very clever one. It made me curious about his background. I didn't ask that night, though.

"That governor of ours make it out of Bellwether all right?"

"As far as I know."

"I suppose most people in here voted for him," he said. "I didn't vote. Don't really matter around here, anyway, going against the grain."

"True enough," I agreed, even though I didn't and took a sip of my drink.

We made some more small talk. Most of it was as boring and fake as that. I was never much good at that sort of chatter—the low stakes nonsense everyone else seemed to learn like riding a bike. Katie was always really good at that, unbelievably charming.

Theodore went back to his bartending duties, and I finished my drink. Not long after his performance ended, the bar started to clear out. I liked when it quieted down. It was more like the dive I knew and loved.

"Enjoying your night?" Theodore asked when there were only a few of us left in the bar.

"Yeah, you could say that." I was getting tired and starting to feel sad about Jeff, honestly. The bourbon wasn't helping. I had consumed plenty by then, perhaps more than I had planned. Though I can't be sure exactly how much.

"Yeah." Theodore slowed down from his fast-paced style of tending bar and stood still in front of me. "It's that time of night. The dark starts to creep in. We do some of our best business as it gets later in the night. Folks start to get real sad and drink a lot more.

"Real pitiful in the true sense. I guess they see us barkeeps as friends and end up spending all their money. Wish I could help, but I'm not too bright and don't always know what to say. That doesn't stop me from giving it my best shot."

"Yeah, well, who really ever does know the right thing to say?" There was an earnest look in his eyes I hadn't seen yet as we held eye contact for a little longer than we ever had before. I felt a heat rush to my face.

Theodore broke eye contact for a moment and rubbed his nose a bit aggressively. I must have given him a funny look because he chuckled and said, "Allergies." I was drunk enough to believe him.

I laughed, too, mostly with him.

He turned away from me for a minute to fill a drink for another customer. I couldn't help but wonder what kind of pain they might be in. I wondered if everyone in here was in some kind of pain—if the ones who left early were, too, or if they were the only ones who weren't. I knew I was in pain, though I wasn't ready to admit it. I could tell Theodore was in pain, too, but I didn't dare tell him I knew. He had dealt me pocket aces, and you never show off that hand.

* * *

The rest of the week after the governor's visit was quite boring, in all honesty. I answered the occasional call—mostly older folks looking to tell me some story about Senator Blythe or passing on a nice message of sympathy to Mayor Wright. I passed all of the notes from those calls on to Christina; I don't know if she gave them to him. I wouldn't have, but that's why I wasn't in charge of making those decisions.

It rained for six days after we had the celebration for the old bastard. It was like the heavens wanted to soak him to decompose his body as fast as they could—get rid of that hate-ridden corpse. Not that I was too religious. I mean, I was religious, but I didn't really believe in some big man in the sky who was going to come and save us all.

There were things in life I couldn't explain. I supposed you could call these miracles. But the world also seemed pretty bad most of the time. I mean, why would they pair Mom up with my father? Hell, why would they let that old bastard Senator Blythe be in such an important position for so long?

So maybe I was never actually that religious. But I'd like to pretend that I was. I think it makes me sound like I was a better person than reality will tell you I was.

Five

In the lobby where I worked in city hall, there was a little cork board where anyone could put up a flyer. Normally, it was ads for bake sales, personals for dog walkers, proselytization for a local church, things like that. None of them were ever that flashy or well designed, but they were at least printed from a computer, so who cares. I didn't really pay it much mind.

The Tuesday after Theodore's little concert— Well, I shouldn't really call it a concert. Concerts have half-decent music and an actual crowd. After Theodore's "set," there was a new flyer on the board. I noticed because it looked like shit. It was a page torn out of a composition notebook, written in what appeared to be black permanent marker.

It read "Show Thursday: Theodore and the Unabombers" with the time and location set as 9 p.m. at the bar.

That idiot, I thought, *made up this flyer and gave himself his very own band name*. I couldn't help but smile.

I didn't make the connection to how he knew where I worked until much later. I thought he was just a stalker at that point. I wondered if he had found other people to play with. I had to go to the show to find out. Maybe he did that intentionally—a curiosity-enticing trap.

* * *

I met Katie the first day of kindergarten. We were seated beside each other on the teacher's chart of desks. I suppose that's how people tend to make friends at that age. Make friends with who you're with and hope it sticks.

Katie was wearing a poofy pink dress. Pink is generally not a color that goes well on redheads. Sure, Molly Ringwald had changed that perspective at one time, but over half a decade had passed since then. Not that Katie had seen *Pretty in Pink* or even knew who Molly Ringwald was. Katie just liked the dress. Katie did what she wanted.

She paired the dress with a pair of muddy sneakers. For all her desire to look fashionable, Katie was also nothing if not industrious. She liked to play, and she liked to play hard, so wearing shoes that matched the dress would have been a nonstarter.

She and I shared a quality in that way. We weren't afraid to play hard, play rough, or get a little muddy. Blue-collar play.

I wore shorts and a T-shirt and sneakers on the first day of school because, even at five, I didn't much care for fashion and just wanted to be able to play unencumbered. Comfort was more important.

With the upbringing I had, I spent most of my time at home outside. Being inside with Mom and my father was not the most fun experience for a young kid, so I was always out splashing in a creek or building a fort or finding some new way to get in trouble.

Katie's family had more money than mine did. That was evident from the fact that they had enough land to have chickens. Not that anyone in Bellwether had money, really, but it was all relative. I never had a pair of name brand shoes, or name brand anything for that matter.

Katie did sometimes. She had a pair of Nike shoes on that first day of school. She had a pair of Nikes, and she had let them get muddy. She was allowed to play in Nikes. I thought she was a millionaire. Really, her mom was a schoolteacher, and her dad was a successful businessman who spent a lot of time traveling.

Her mom ran the homestead. She was the farmer and the cook and the cleaner and the disciplinarian and the handywoman. Her dad would bring her gifts when he came back from the city and clearly loved her and her mom more than life itself. Not that life wasn't complicated; he was gone a lot, and that was hard, but I never doubted that Katie's dad's love was real. That was rare in my mind.

When Christmas came when we were in first grade, Beanie Babies were all the rage. I mean everyone had to have one of those things. They weren't *that* expensive, really, but by my family's standards they were. Mom, God bless her, scraped up a little cash to get me what I called an "Almost-Beanie Baby." It wasn't a Beanie Baby by name, but it looked just like one. It was a little brown monkey.

I loved that thing until I went to school the first Monday back and heard other kids talking about the real-deal Beanie Babies they had gotten. Then my little monkey became embarrassing to me.

I confided in Katie that I hadn't gotten a real Beanie Baby, but a "fake one." I thought she would make fun of me—or worse, not want to be my friend anymore. She didn't, though. She said she was sure it was still really cute and that it meant my mom really cared that she had tried to get me the next closest thing.

A couple of days later, Katie came in and sat down beside me. She unzipped her book bag and handed me a brand-new Beanie Baby. Patti the Platypus. I didn't know what the hell a platypus was. I didn't care. That was the nicest thing anyone had ever done for me. I loved Katie that day. I wish I had told her.

Either way, that solidified our friendship forever, and I wanted to spend the rest of time trying to prove to Katie that she meant as much to me as I clearly did to her.

Patti and the monkey still sit on my desk, under my computer monitor, in the office of the mayor of Bellwether.

* * *

"Jesse," Christina said. "The private family funeral for Senator Blythe is going to be on Sunday here in town. You don't need to attend, but do you mind getting a bouquet of flowers for Mayor Wright to bring?"

"Sure thing. Is there anything specific he wants?"

"No, he doesn't know he's bringing them yet." She was standing in the doorway to Mayor Wright's office, behind and to the left of my desk. "But it would be nice for him to place some at the grave after the burial, I think. Just something simple and classy will be all we need, dear."

If I was someone who had an important job and was busy all the time, I would've bought a dozen tulips and mailed it in. I was not busy. Work was not normally as busy as it had been the last week and a half. I decided to buy flowers with a pointed meaning. No one else would know, but I would. My knowing was worth it.

I spent, unbeknownst to my employer—or any of the folks on the other end of calls I answered—several hours researching flower meanings that day.

I went with a bouquet of dark crimson roses, to symbolize mourning. Normal, classy, fair. Sprinkled into the bouquet, I added geranium flowers. Victorian symbolism dictates that geranium flowers signify stupidity and foolishness.

It was fucking mean, and I knew it. I meant it. I still do.

Cole William Barnhill

Thirty-three terms in office and the old bastard didn't solve one of our goddamn problems.

I was sitting on my couch until past eight on Thursday night. It was deeply quiet in the house. When it's that quiet, it's easy to just sit there in it and experience the physical extravagances of emotions.

After Jeff left, I found it gradually harder and harder to stand up off the couch at night. Some nights I just slept there. Some nights it was one or two before I went to the bed, which now felt way too empty. I had always shared it. I didn't love him, but the void was heavy, and it took out some of my soul. It was as if I became glued to the couch, and no summonable level of willpower could get me up until the ache let me.

It was so quiet.

I thought about Jeff and how I hated his face. I thought about Theodore and his cooked little grin.

I got up and went out the door before I let myself think too much about it. I looked like garbage, I'm sure. I didn't check my hair. Didn't check my makeup. I still had on my dull work clothes. Not exactly sexy. But Jeff wasn't my husband anymore. I had no one to impress.

I thought about the whiskey I would order. I worried if I would be able to find a seat at the bar. That held me in the driveway for a moment. Key in hand, staring out of the windshield at nothing in particular. The flaking

46

paint on the siding was a void of a different kind where thoughts went to be planted.

I took a deep breath and started the car. I didn't plan to drink enough that I wouldn't be able to drive home. I never really did drink that much. I did some, early in my relationship with Jeff. We would go out with people we called friends and get drunk. Jeff still called them friends. I didn't. They weren't.

The bar was loud enough to hear it from outside as I approached. I hadn't missed Theodore's set. It sounded about as bad as it had the week before. Although different songs this time was a sign of *some* improvement.

There was almost no one inside when I opened the door, though. There was a couple at the bar who looked to be trying in vain to ignore Theodore. It was a first date. It appeared to also be a last date. Can't win 'em all.

Theodore was playing rock songs I didn't recognize. This was the up-tempo part of his set. He could have written the songs himself, but I wasn't sure. I just knew I didn't know them, and I knew they didn't sound incredible.

I got a drink. A double. More bourbon. The drive of the song, and the roughness of Theodore's voice made me drink it faster than usual. I ordered another.

He closed his set with a couple of country songs I vaguely recognized. He may not have been good, but he had plenty of range in the types of things he played. I couldn't quite place the songs, but I knew these weren't originals. As bad as he was, I sort of wanted him to keep going. The music was, for all of its shakiness, consistent, and that made it easy to drink to.

But he did finish. Not soon enough for the couple. They left during his last song. The woman looked ready to be driven home. I assumed the man wouldn't be getting a goodnight kiss. Even if she were attracted to him, she would never be able to see his face again without thinking of Theodore's gaudy and not-so-finely honed vocal performance.

If only I had an excuse like that after my first date with Jeff. Our first date was quieter, though. It didn't end with a goodnight kiss, but it did end with sex. It was good enough for me to see him again. I was lonely then.

Theodore sat down beside me after he finished playing. I tried to act cool and not watch him the whole way over. I was on my third drink. I was not sober. I wasn't drunk yet, though, just tipsy. Honestly, I couldn't tell the difference—it had been a long time since I had even been tipsy.

"Howdy, stranger." He grinned his stupid grin as he sat down. He motioned to the bartender, his coworker, for another round. He inhaled hard and turned to me. "You saw my billboard, I guess."

"Playing it a little fast and loose with the word *billboard* aren't you there, fella?" I prodded him.

"I'll have you know I spent thirty minutes on that thing." He smirked. "Spent most of it finding a marker, but it counts."

"Well, it did the job," I told him. "If only because I wanted to see if you had actually found bandmates or if you were just trying to get me to come by."

He leaned back on his barstool and chuckled. He put a guitar pick down in front of us.

"Only bandmate I need right here." He tapped it. "This and my guitar there. Make me sound not too bad, I think."

"Well, you certainly played an interesting variety tonight. I would've liked to hear some originals, though." I winked. I never wink. I was deep into my next drink. I was pretty drunk.

"That's a tough ask." He finished his drink and gestured for another round. "God didn't gift me with the best words. I just use the ones other folks already came up with. Easier that way."

I laughed a little harder than I should have. The joke wasn't that funny. Yeah, I was definitely drunk.

Six

I had my head down with my eyes closed. I was in the part of drunk where reality was starting to slip from my mind and come in waves. I had feeling in my body, but I'm not sure that my brain was in it.

I felt a hand on mine. It held the outside of my palm and squeezed for comfort. I was sixteen again and at Marianne's funeral. Mom was back and about to tell me she loved me for the last time. This time I wanted to say it back. I would get to say it and mean it, and it would save her, and she would leave my father, and our lives would be great.

I opened my eyes, and I was at a bar. Theodore wasn't smiling but his eyes were as blue as ever. Blue enough to cover the bloodshot whites and they welcomed me to come inside. His face was earnest. He was the warmth the world needed the week after Mom died. But I was pretty drunk.

I wasn't sure how long I had my head down or eyes closed, but it was long enough. I hoped Theodore hadn't seen any pain on my face. But I didn't know, I was pretty drunk.

Theodore asked the other bartender for a couple of waters. He made me finish mine as he finished his. We sat there for a while trying to sober up. He wanted me, and he wanted me to want him. He wanted me to be able to consent. I wanted him, too. But I was pretty drunk.

"Can I take you home?" he asked.

I nodded.

"I need you to tell me," he said.

"I want you to take me home," I told him.

"Okay," he whispered.

I remember what happened next, but you don't get to know. I was pretty drunk, but I know he was better than Jeff.

Seven

It was junior year of high school when Mom died. I had thought about moving out a lot growing up. Life was hard, obviously, and my father made it harder, but I had to stay for Mom. Running away probably wouldn't have solved my issues, but it certainly would have made Mom's worse. I don't know what my father would have done to her, but the thought of it reminds me that there might be worse things in life than death.

Staying around for someone else is a hard way to live, but still, I didn't really know where else I would go, anyway. It's not like I had money for an apartment, or even a job. I was just a seventeen-year-old trying to make it through my last years of school. I was just smart enough to know how much I didn't know anything.

I had no intention of going to college. No one from Bellwether went to college. Some people went to the community college down the mountain. But those people were either destined for some kind of greatness or disillusioned about their own goodness.

I didn't want to go to school anymore, though. I wanted to work. I wanted a job, and I wanted to work so I could make money and move out and take Mom with me.

I had to take Mom with me, and I really did believe she and I could have a better life somewhere together. I carried that dream for as long as I could, but perhaps there is some truth to the phrase *It's the hope that kills you*. Maybe it's just a certain kind of hope—a tangibly untrue kind. The kind of hope that tells you at seventeen that you can escape the cycle of misery that your father seemed destined to carry on.

But I don't know. I don't think Mom ever felt any kind of hope—reasonable or otherwise. I think she had just accepted, maybe even before I came along, a desolate sort of lonesome life. Maybe it wasn't the hope that killed her, but the impossibility of it.

I mentioned that it snowed a lot in the period just after Mom died, but until that point, it had been a normal, maybe even mild winter. We had some flurries and the peaks got sugar coatings occasionally, but it was January, and we hadn't had any major snows. Bellwether was only good for one or two real big ones in any given year, anyway.

It was the first day back from winter break. I had been home for almost a month over the holiday, and it had been, as much as it could be in that house, nice. My father didn't beat anyone, and he wasn't too belligerent most of the time. A product of having two of us to spread his ire over, maybe.

Mom spent most of her time in the kitchen. She baked a lot that winter, I remember that. She made everything she could to try to keep my father happy. I wondered if maybe she was trying to poison him. I wished that she had. Years of being beaten down by everyone who pretends to love you will make you cower. Mom cowered, but I know she would've given anything for my father to go before her.

The first day back to school something snapped in her. She was unusually quiet that morning. She made me breakfast but didn't speak. I wish she had.

Apparently, she had something of an episode after I left. If Marianne's dying tore her in half, the end of the near-blissful holiday tore her in quarters. I don't know what was said. I can't imagine she said anything that bad, anything truly offensive. But my father didn't need to hear anything that bad—the reality of the situation wasn't what drove him.

Whatever happened, he hit Mom. He hit her with an open hand, and he hit her hard. The mark was gone by the time the ambulance came. I didn't know any of the details, really, until after I had started working for Mayor Wright. I had access to the police report through the computer on my desk.

My father hit Mom, and it was the final straw. Mom just couldn't do it anymore—the last thread of her will to continue tore.

She went into their bedroom and locked the door. She took my father's 12-gauge out of the gun safe and swallowed the barrel. That was a picture wrap on Carline Strotherton. It took thirty-seven years, but she finally got to make a decision on her own. I was glad, to be honest. I miss Mom. I wish we could've had the life she deserved, but she also deserved a little peace.

* * *

One of the duties of a small-town mayor is attending seemingly trivial events. Ribbon cuttings, building dedications, retirement ceremonies, banquets for organizations—things like that. It's probably even more important in a small town where retail politics rule all and everyone knows the mayor personally—or at least thinks that they do.

Mayor Wright went to a lot of these things. I didn't always go to them, but sometimes they had me tag along. Most of the time they were boring affairs, but they were important to the folks hosting them.

The next Monday morning brought about another event that Mayor Wright had agreed to go to. I thought it was a little beneath him, but he wanted to go. He said it was the right thing to do, the honorable thing to do. He wanted to do what was right even if it looked meaningless or felt like a gesture of futility. I went along with it because I didn't have a choice. What was I going to say, anyway?

Don't go Mr. Mayor. It's pretty stupid. That wasn't my role—though I'm not sure that was actually anyone's role.

It was a bench dedication for an Eagle Scout project. Some high school kid had built a wooden bench in the park for his community service requirement, and they were, I don't know, opening it? I'm not sure that you really *open* a bench, but there we were, all gathered around this wooden bench that had already been there for a couple of days and had probably already been sat on.

The kid said a few words. His scout leader said a few words then thanked Mayor Wright for coming. Mayor Wright generously thanked them for inviting him. I really didn't think that they genuinely thought he would come—they just invited him as a courtesy, hoping he might come out, I guess. Well, he did.

Mayor Wright said a few words. How beautiful the bench was, how great an addition it was to the park, what a great contribution to the community it was—stuff like that. I thought it was bullshit, at least it would have been if I was the one speaking, but as always, he was being earnest. It wasn't in Mayor Wright's wheelhouse to be anything but earnest.

A photographer snapped a couple of pictures of the kid and Mayor Wright and the scout leader and the kid's family in all different arrangements. I never understood pictures like that. No way this kid's parents were going to frame all of the pictures of them with people they didn't know—hell, they probably didn't frame the picture of them with their son. But everyone smiles gladly for the pictures all the same. Perhaps the memory of having taken the photo was more important than the photo itself.

After everyone had said their little blurbs and posed pictures were taken, the kid invited Mayor Wright to be the "first" person to sit on the bench.

Mayor Wright smiled at the camera as they took pictures of him sitting down and in slow motion falling clean through the seat of the bench. The wood slats just came completely unattached, so there was Mayor Wright, folded up like a lawn chair, knees held up by the front beam, back held up by the backrest of the seat, ass firmly on the ground.

Apparently, the bench truly had not been sat on before him. Or someone very, very light had sat on it. The kid was, I am sure, mortified. But there was my boss, crying laughing.

"Well, that's one way to do it," he said in self-deprecation through his giggles. "Might want to delete those pictures there, partner."

Someone helped him to his feet. The kid had his hand on his forehead. He was clearly embarrassed. I felt bad for him. He had spent some real time on this bench, and the mayor had come out for his big moment, and the damn thing broke. I would've been devastated.

Mayor Wright put a hand on his shoulder.

"Ain't nothing but a thing, bud." He smiled. "How about I help you get it fixed up since I was the one who broke it?"

The kid sort of faked a smile and tried to laugh through some tears.

"Sure," he muttered.

"Still got your tools in your truck?" I don't know how Mayor Wright knew that this kid drove a truck, but he did. It made me believe Mayor Wright knew everything about everyone in town—and maybe he did. The kid nodded, halved a smile, and went to retrieve his toolbox.

Mayor Wright spent the next hour, honest to God, with no cameras pointed at him, helping this kid reconstruct his bench. He showed him some new techniques to make it stronger than before and to make sure it would last. He made plans—which Christina wrote down to schedule officially—to come back out to the park to help the kid treat the bench so it would be weatherproof.

No one wrote about it in the paper. He didn't embarrass the kid, he even made him smile and shake it off. He didn't earn a single new vote—that kid couldn't even vote for him for another two or three years.

That was just Mayor Wright being Mayor Wright. It was a hell of a thing.

* * *

Early in high school, Katie and I got a little more freedom to explore town. It wasn't explicitly given by our folks, but we were a little more comfortable pushing the boundaries—and maybe they were a little more comfortable letting us—and we had already been given freedom to bike around and play since we were little. Bellwether was a small town, and it was the early 2000s, remember. A different time.

We had reached the age where we were looking for trouble. We never would've admitted that, but the way we explored told on us. We liked sneaking onto construction sites and jumping fences. Going onto folks' properties and getting chased by their dogs. *I don't have to outrun the dog, just you*, Katie would always tell me as she tore off ahead of me. I never did get bitten, though.

One day at school, Katie told me about an old fire road she had heard about. It was off a little greenway on the north side of town. I'd been that way before but couldn't place the road she was talking about. It was overgrown, she told me, but if you knew where to look, you could still find it.

Katie seemed unusually excited, so I was on board. It didn't take a whole lot to get me on board, but when Katie got excited about something, she was normally right. She seemed to think that the old fire road went on a good way up into the forest and that there might be some abandoned stuff up the hill we could explore. I had no reason not to believe her.

Everyone knew the new fire road. It was on the opposite side of the mountain and went up the hill to the peak. Forest fires weren't real common in the area—at least back then—but the road had to be there just in case. People camped up near the top sometimes, so emergencies did happen from time to time. Mostly snakebites and rolled ankles.

The "new" road was put in before I was born, so I had never even considered that there might be an old one. I had been up to the peak plenty of times. It was a nice view up there, but the forest was thick, so I'm not sure I would've been able to see the old road if I *was* looking for it.

Up until high school, Katie and I had ridden the bus to school every day. After middle school, as a part of our newfound freedoms, we got permission to ride our bikes to school. It was only a couple of blocks so it wasn't a big ask—we could have walked—but it felt like a big measure of freedom to us. We felt like adults. We felt like we ruled the world. Never mind that a lot of kids biked or walked to the high school. There were only a couple of buses in Bellwether due to there being only one high school, so if you lived close to the high school, it was sometimes simply faster to walk than to wait on the bus all morning.

School got out at 2:45. My father got home around six o'clock most days and liked for me to be home before him. Mom didn't care. Still, it wasn't uncommon for me to stay at Katie's house until dinner time, around eight o'clock, or vice versa. Katie's parents never really worried about where we were at all. As long as she came home at some point, they were fine with it. They still, perhaps in folly, believed that small towns were always safe—that everyone's folks looked after everyone's kids.

Suffice it to say we felt confident messing around town for a few hours after school. We had mild permission to, and we rarely got in trouble for getting home too late, and we didn't care when we did. My father would threaten me, but I was fifteen with an ego the size of Texas—he didn't scare me none anymore.

It was a warm day. Fall hadn't fully set in yet. The sun was out so people were out. We had company the whole way as we rode toward the greenway. People piddled out as we went, arriving at their homes or ending their afternoon exercises. I was sweating pretty good from chasing Katie—she was more athletic than me—when she put a foot on the ground and swung her head around to see if there were people nearby. There weren't.

"We're here." She flashed an excited smile at me.

The trees were huge and green and cast shadows over the greenway. It was still, but some birds were chirping. The grasses and saplings were grown up along the path—I didn't know what the hell I was supposed to be looking at. Katie looked around again to make sure we were alone then gestured for me to follow her. She picked up her bike and lifted it over the thickest row of plant life.

It was a little bit clearer past the first thicket, but I still didn't really see a "road" to speak of. Still, I picked up my bike and followed. Katie leaned her bike against a tree and skipped with joy a few strides into the woods. Past the first rows of trees—there wasn't any old growth there—the woods opened up a bit and showed us two ruts with a line of grasses and wildfires. Sure enough, a road. An old one, still largely grown over—trees growing up trying to punch through the gravel—but it was there.

"Here we are." Katie dramatically gestured with her arm to the road before us.

"As it were." I was still a bit skeptical.

"Oh, come on." She picked her bike back up and hopped on. "It'll be great."

I hopped on my bike and followed Katie as she tore up the road through the woods, cutting her legs up on the needling thorns of fruit-bearing blackberry bushes as she ripped through the brush.

Not far up the hill, we came upon a bridge. It was about as wide as the path—not wide enough for two cars to pass, certainly. It was made of railway ties over large metal trusses. There was chicken wire attached to metal pipes on the sides, I guess to prevent people from jumping off—as if people couldn't just hop over the railing. I wasn't sure what the point was, really.

The railway ties were aged but not eroding. The bridge seemed sturdy, but Katie got off her bike, so I followed. She took a few steps out and turned back to me.

"Seems sturdy enough." She stomped her foot on the thick wood. "Let's go."

She walked her bike across the bridge, and I followed behind. The trees had grown over so there wasn't much to see from the bridge save for the trickle of a creek below. I was surprised I hadn't known it was up there, but then again, I hadn't even known the road was up there.

I looked through the gaps in the ties as we walked. I could just make out the water below, mirroring the speckled sunlight which broke through the gaps in the trees. The shade made it cool in the woods, and the water made it cooler. I looked up, and Katie was already across and mounting her bike.

We biked for a while. I never wore a watch, so I don't know how long. Katie was the one responsible for making sure we got home on time. She had a super hero wristwatch her grandmom gave her for Christmas. She could tell time better than me because of it.

We went, I'm not sure, maybe a mile up the trail. It certainly felt like a substantial distance.

For the most part the road stayed the same. Thick forest on either side of us, thick grasses and weeds and small saplings in the center, and gravel peeking through the ruts of what used to be the fire road.

We came upon a building. I saw it first. I'm pretty sure Katie would have gone right on past it if I hadn't said something. It was a white, two-story brick structure. It looked to be a house. It was largely covered by vines; moss on the roof and foliage covering any walkway that may have once existed.

There was no door. There was a single doorway, on the right side of the building facing the road on the first floor. A window was beside it. There were a couple of windows on what was apparently the second floor. There was no glass in any of the windows, and I could see, even from a distance, that plants were growing in the floorboards of the upper floor.

I got off my bike and waited for Katie to come back to meet me. She hopped off hers and flipped her kickstand. She tapped her foot on the first row of taller undergrowth to check for snakes. Seeing none, she walked in toward the house. I followed, matching her steps to avoid getting in the grass too much. I was, and still am, afraid of ticks. There were plenty out in those woods.

Katie stopped in the doorway of the house before entering. She felt the frame to see if it was sturdy and looked around at the downstairs floor to make sure it was intact. It was. It was a single concrete slab with hardwood floors laid over top. The wood had started to break down and fall apart, and there were patches where the wood was gone entirely, and you could see the concrete underneath. It was grown over substantially with moss, but no trees or larger plants had managed to break through yet.

Katie walked into the center of the room and stood there looking around, taking it all in. I followed her in and walked a loop around the walls. There wasn't any graffiti. That was surprising to me. The house seemed long abandoned; I assumed someone would have gone out there at some point to hang out and fuck around. Instead, it seemed mostly untouched.

There were stairs along the wall heading upstairs. I walked over to the base of them and peeked up. There wasn't much to see—a rotting ceiling and rickety-looking steps. I tapped the bottom step with the toe of my shoe, and it didn't move. It didn't look steady, though, so I didn't go up.

I looked out the missing window and noticed the sun was lower in the kaleidoscopic trees.

"We should probably head out." I turned to Katie. She was looking out of an opposite window.

"Yeah," she said. "But we should come back this weekend!"

I nodded and headed out to my bike. We got home before the streetlights came on. Home even before my father returned.

Eight

Monday morning at the mayor's office was, as usual, spent lazily catching up on the messages from the weekend. I was wading through angry and concerned and complimentary and disdained voicemails when Mayor Wright came out of his office and tapped his knuckles on my desk to get my attention.

He always did that whenever he needed me and I was using the phone because I always jumped when someone tapped me on the shoulder. He didn't like that. I didn't like it, either, to be fair.

"Busy?"

I shook my head. "Just catching up on messages from the weekend."

"Anything interesting?"

"Just the usual," I told him and hung up on the phone as the message I was listening to ended.

It was a mom complaining about someone driving too fast through her neighborhood. She wanted speed bumps installed. The roads were cracked to shit, but yeah, I'm sure there was money in the city budget for new speed bumps. She would get a call back from Christina later. Christina was kind and convincing enough to handle those kinds of calls. Those kinds of calls were not close to important enough to end up on Mayor Wright's desk.

"Well, I'm bored." He chuckled. His smile cracked through his beard, and his eyes squinted. He looked sort of like a redneck Santa Claus, just with a more well-kept beard. "I don't have anything important going on. Why don't you take a break and have a coffee with me?"

"Um, sure," I agreed and stood up. I had a pang in my stomach that I may have done something wrong, but I had no idea what I could have possibly done. Nothing, apparently.

"You've been loyal to me for a while now, Jesse," he told me. "But I'm not a dummy. I know you don't agree with everything I do and say. I want you to tell me, honestly, what do you disagree with me about the most?"

I wasn't prepared for that question. Obviously, I disagreed with Mayor Wright on plenty. He was relatively conservative—though I suppose he was a centrist by technical standards—and I was a liberal.

But being the mayor of a small town, it wasn't as much of an issue. He mostly did common sense and ceremonial stuff. The town council did some wild, backward stuff sometimes, but it's not like he could stop them. Not to mention, Mayor Wright was never very outward about a lot of social issues. I didn't even know what he believed on some things, to be honest.

"I know there's something you feel passionately about." He pressed gently. "You could answer the phone anywhere, and you're plenty qualified to do a lot more than that. Not to mention you could get paid plenty more working just about anywhere else. But you're here. I can't imagine that it's only because we posted a want ad."

I thought about it for a moment. Perhaps in part of my mind I had come to work there because I wanted to do *something* with my life after watching so many people do nothing with theirs. Working for the mayor felt like something, I guess.

"I guess, and I say this with all possible respect . . ." He nodded understandingly, urging me to continue. I worried he would get mad at me for what I believed. I needed to keep my job. But he was asking. So I continued, "Sir, you've got things totally backwards on drugs."

"How do you mean?" He seemed surprised, but mostly genuinely curious.

"Well, Mr. Mayor, you're trying to put finger bandages on bullet holes," I told him. "You want to get drugs off the streets, and you're trying to get people to stop using drugs, right? Well, you're trying to do that by force. You want to arrest people who have or use drugs, and you want to confiscate drugs."

He nodded.

"That's a perfectly logical idea in theory, but it just isn't reality. I've been around drug users my whole life, and no laws and no amount of pressure from the police is going to stop folks from using drugs. The only way to get people off of drugs is to treat them for drug addiction. Treat it like the illness it is, and you've got a shot."

Mayor Wright nodded again. "Okay," he said slowly. He seemed to be trying to take it all in.

I continued, "But if you try to regulate by force then folks are going to get drugs from sketchier sources, and God knows what is going to be in the drugs. That's how you get folks overdosing because their stuff was spiked.

"If you chill out on criminalizing drugs and make sure that people who are addicted are using safe drugs, then you can treat people while keeping them alive at the same time. The harder you push on criminalization instead of treatment, the more it will push drug users underground, the less safe it will be, the more users you will get because more folks will get hooked on more illicit stuff, and the more crime you will generate."

Mayor Wright sat and thought for a minute before he said anything.

"I hear you," he said. "And what you're saying all makes sense . . . I guess folks in this town just expect me to be tough on crime, and I'm inclined to agree with 'em."

"That's fair, but I don't think you're preventing crime." I pushed back. "If anything, you're just creating more. When folks have to go underground to do drugs, they're going to be inclined to commit other crimes while they're at it. If what you're doing is already illegal, is already in the depths of secrecy, what's one more illegal act, you know?"

Mayor Wright stroked his beard and made a thinking *hmm*.

"I see your point," he said. He looked me in the eyes. He always looked folks in the eyes when he really meant something. "I'm not going to go as far as to say I agree with you just yet, but I sure will give it a long think. I appreciate you talking with me, Jesse."

Duty called for the mayor of Bellwether, as Christina had been lurking in the doorway behind me for a while. Mayor Wright stood up and left me alone with my coffee. I felt my body relax. I didn't realize how much I had tensed up while I was talking—it was quite nerve-racking to be that honest with Mayor Wright, especially about something that we disagreed on.

I felt pretty sure nothing would change. Why would it? The war on drugs had been raging all my life— "Just Say No" and all of that bullshit—it wasn't going to change now, and Mayor Wright certainly wasn't going to be the one to change it. But I appreciated him hearing me out. I respected the hell out of him for listening thoughtfully to someone make the case for something that one, he disagreed with and two, he had almost certainly already thought plenty about.

It wasn't like Bellwether didn't have a drug problem or that it was anything new—everywhere in Appalachia did. You can't be a mayor anywhere without having thought about your position on drugs—and thought about it thoroughly. But Mayor Wright listened to me all the same. I felt better for it, and I felt better about working for him for it.

* * *

I hadn't seen Theodore since we spent the night together. Not that I was avoiding him, but we hadn't made plans, and I hadn't been to the bar. I wasn't sure if I meant anything to him. I'd had one-night stands before. I imagined that he had, too. I wasn't sure if I wanted him to mean anything to me, either.

It's not like he had come by work at any point to see me, either. He obviously knew where I worked. If he really wanted to see me, he could have. So I sort of resigned myself to the one night with Theodore being just that: one good night.

Friday afternoon I was wrapping up my work, ready to go home for the weekend. It had been an uneventful week. Mayor Wright didn't even stay in the office too late most days. I was sort of mailing it in for five o'clock so I could go home for the weekend when the door opened.

It wasn't often that folks physically came into the office without an appointment. I didn't have an appointment listed on my schedule, and when that's the case you never really know what's walking through that door. More than once I had seen people burst into the office and come raging hot demanding to talk to the mayor. Normally it was because they didn't pay their water bill or got a parking ticket or something. You know, things the mayor doesn't control *at all*.

Theodore didn't come in yelling or striding to me to get in my face. He slid in the door softly and flashed his signature grin at me. He was more subdued than usual, but still himself.

"Howdy stranger," he said.

I looked up at him and couldn't hide my smile.

"Oh, hey there, Unabomber." I realized that was an odd thing to say out loud in the mayor's office, but no one else was around.

"I thought you'd forgotten about me," he said, leaning so he sat sideways on the edge of my desk.

"I could say the same thing to you." I tried to poke. "But then again, I guess I was the one who kept on coming to you."

Theodore smiled real big at me. He knew he had me.

"True enough." He paused and ran his fingers over his top lip and chin. "Well, Miss Jesse, I come with a peace offering and a plan. If you want it, of course."

I closed out the window I had been looking at on my computer and turned off my monitor. I always did that when it was time to leave. I liked to start completely fresh the next day. It was rare I ever had projects to work on that were significant enough that I couldn't close them out at the end of the day—I didn't like to take that work, that thought, home with me at the end of the day.

I took my time before responding to Theodore. I wanted to play coy. Messing with him gave me a pleasure I hadn't known in a while. I smirked at him and leaned back in my chair, crossing my legs.

"What is it you have in mind?"

"You ever seen a bunch of poor folks burn off all their stress by beating the shit out of each other?" he asked. That wasn't what I was expecting from him, and I genuinely had no idea where the hell he was going with it. I played along to humor what was clearly a thought-through plan.

"Can't say that I have." This was true.

"Well, I do think it's something we all ought to see in our lives," he said, standing up. "And it's Friday. Best damn night of the week for it."

Theodore and I had slept together once, but we hadn't really known each other that long. This was an odd way to proposition a . . . I guess, date? There were no details, and it sounded quite sketchy, frankly. I probably should have said no or made up an excuse to not go. But there was something about that grin. I trusted him even though I maybe shouldn't have, and I agreed to go.

"And what is *it*?" I said as I stood up and put my hands on my desk. I felt awkward as I did it, but it was like I didn't have control of my own body anymore. I just flowed into the moment.

"You ever see those old tattoos of boxers that ole sailors used to get? Well, it's sort of like that, 'cept bare knuckled and it's poor folks, and it ain't even sort of sanctioned by nobody." He leaned back and laughed with his hand on his belly. It reminded me how much taller he was than me. I liked that about him. I also liked how his drawl got more country when he got excited about something. I never had a "real" southern accent, but he sure did.

I wasn't totally sold on what we were going to, but it had been a slow week, and I was looking for a good time. I was willing to give it a try.

* * *

Saturdays in Bellwether were ours. Sundays were for our parents—chores, church, paying for whatever trouble we got into on Saturday. We almost always had some sort of extra chore to do to make up for our Saturday sins.

A couple of weeks after we had found the house, Katie wanted to go back. She had the idea of bringing some friends back and having a party. I thought it would be unsafe, but I didn't care. I knew how to get out of sketchy situations, and if people I didn't call my friends didn't know how to get out, who was I to worry on them?

I slept over with Katie on Friday night so I didn't have to tell my folks where I was going. Not that they would have cared, anyway, but any chance to avoid the conversation.

I didn't have a plan for how the day would go. I assumed Katie did. Katie always had something in mind. I was just a passenger in her grand adventures.

Sure enough, she got us up early. She had already made sandwiches for us to bring for lunch by the time I was up and dressed. She threw them in her book bag. Not the best storage method for a sandwich which should be kept cool, but what else was she going to do? What's a little food poisoning between friends?

By midmorning we were on our bikes and off to the greenway. It dawned on me that we weren't bringing any party supplies, but again, I left it to Katie and assumed she had it handled. She said that most people wouldn't show up until midafternoon, and we were just going to set up.

"What's there to set up in a run-down abandoned house? I asked.

"You'll see," she assured me.

It was Katie's movie, and I was just a supporting character.

Maybe it was because we had gone there before and already knew the way, but it felt like the ride to the house was not nearly as long as it had been the first time. The trestle slowed us down, but in between, we were flying through the woods. We made it to the house well before lunch, and to my surprise, we weren't alone.

There was already a bike leaning against the exterior wall of the house. I was sure it had not been there the first time we went up there, and it looked new. The hairs on my neck stood up when I saw that bike, and I stopped in my tracks.

"Hold on, Katie. I think someone else is in there." I grabbed her arm and stopped her.

Katie reached across with her other arm and loosened my grip. She grabbed my hand and squeezed it gently.

"It's okay!" she said. "It's just Jimi—he's here to help us set up."

Jimi was one of our classmates. His parents insisted he be called James, but he loved Hendrix and hated his parents. So he went with Jimi, and we all obliged him. Except for our principal. She was friends with Jimi's parents, apparently, so he was James to her. Shockingly, Jimi did not get along particularly well with our principal and was a frequent flier of sorts in detention.

Anyway, Jimi was a good guy, I thought. I didn't know him that well, I concede, and as a result I didn't know a whole lot about him. Katie knew everyone, though. There was no one she wasn't friends with. I generally trusted people whom Katie liked on principle, or at least I tried to.

"Hey dudes!" Jimi had heard us talking and poked his head through the door. He had an easy smile and big white teeth. He was the kind of guy who was blessed with never needing to go to a dentist, much less an orthodontist.

"Hey Jimi! How's it going?" Katie answered and walked toward the house. I followed. As much as I trusted her, this felt more like of a leap of faith than the usual sort of buy-in into the things she got us into.

Jimi didn't say anything until we got inside. That made me nervous, but I took a deep breath and exhaled hard while trying to keep it quiet. I had to remember that I loved and trusted Katie and liked and trusted what I knew about him.

"It's going great. I found some old plywood out back and made a little makeshift table out of it to put drinks on." Jimi gestured to a God-knows-how-old piece of plywood on top of what appeared to be two rusted-out oil drums. Jimi had an older brother who had gotten him a twenty-four pack of Keystone Light. They were set out on the table. They were distinctly not cold. I was not inclined to partake. If desperation had a name, it would be warm Keystone in an abandoned house. We were young, though, so I guess that made it less pathetic.

"Excellent work!" Katie gave him a hug. I followed suit.

"Sally is bringing a boombox to play some music," Jimi continued his explanation/tour of the house that Katie and I had discovered. It was odd seeing someone else take ownership of something I felt my own personal ownership of. "I think she's got a bunch of CDs, but I'm hoping we can get some radio signal up here."

Wishful thinking there, I thought.

People started to find their way up to the house over the next couple of hours. I was impressed that Katie had given good enough directions that it seemed not too many people got lost. That wouldn't have been the case had I been the planner. The house was not, obviously, on the beaten path.

A lot of the people who arrived brought cases of other various cheap beers. None of them cold, none of them of any sort of quality, but all of them containing enough alcohol to make people forget how bad they tasted. That was, I suppose, part of the pleasure of underage drinking. Not drinking to enjoy, drinking to forget.

Sally Kennedy, as promised, was one of the first to show up after us. She joked that she was a long lost relative of Jack Kennedy from when he campaigned through West Virginia. The story went that Jack, in his inability to keep it in his pants, had gotten some relative of hers pregnant.

The story wasn't true, of course. Her raven hair gave her away. And her family tree, I'm sure. But it was a fun story, and folks didn't spend enough time on it to analyze its merits.

Sally looked tired when she rolled up. The ride up the hill had to take its toll on someone—it had spared Jimi. Sally took the full brunt of the climb, her hair frizzed out as if she'd just stepped from a sauna. She looked rough, but she came bearing musical reinforcements.

The boombox she brought did have an antenna, but it was small, and I was fairly certain it was not designed to get signal out in the woods. Luckily, Sally brought CDs, too.

Jimi was going to give it the old college try, though. He was bound and determined to get a radio signal, and he came armed with a toolbox hitched on to his bike. "Always be prepared," he said. I actually liked that aspect of Jimi—it was a good rule to live by. My father always said never to leave home without a knife. I didn't.

From his toolbox he grabbed some pliers and tape. He used some scrap wire he found in the woods to fashion a slightly longer antenna. While he worked, he played CDs and only vaguely looked over as more and more of our classmates showed up. I recognized most of them.

After a couple of hours, Jimi rose and announced to the party that his antenna was ready and prepared everyone to revel in the glory of his creation and all of the sure-to-be plentiful radio stations we could now reach. He flipped the boombox over to FM radio, and it unleashed the most staticky, popping radio signal I'd ever heard. Still, it was a signal, as it were. He was real proud of himself.

A guy I didn't recognize helped Jimi, and a couple of tweaks later, the raggedy antenna finally found a clean signal, and a rock station came through as clear as it ever would. It was poppy, but it was music, and it was variety. The partygoers, who were at this point, well . . . not sober, went wild.

I didn't care, though. I wasn't a huge partier, and the event had gone well beyond where I thought it would. There were way too many people in that damned house. *My* house, I thought of it.

I tried to have fun. I honestly did, but I just couldn't reach the emotion. Katie danced with people she knew, but I didn't. I mostly just watched. She seemed to be having fun without me, which felt, if anything, isolating. The party was not mine.

I didn't leave with Katie the day we had that first party in the house. I left when I'd had enough. It was late in the afternoon and folks were starting to get properly drunk. I was fine with that. I didn't have a problem with alcohol or people partying. I wasn't even holding a grudge about so many people coming to a place I thought could be a sanctuary for just Katie and me.

I left when I saw a guy whom I didn't even recognize do a line of coke off Jimi's makeshift table. Forget for a second the drugs of it all, there's no way that table was remotely sanitary. Although a guy doing coke off a sketchy table at a sketchy house in the middle of the woods has probably already looked away from sanitation at some point in his life. The cleanliness of the surface was not the deal-breaker for him.

Well, I should clarify, just one guy doing coke at a party wasn't the line for me leaving. The final straw for me was when Jimi took part, and Katie was cheering him on. I didn't know if Katie was next in line or just a bystander to it all—a negligent cheerleader in the ill-thought crime ongoing.

It didn't matter; I didn't stay. I left without my best friend. I left feeling like I was no longer Katie's best friend, but she was, by process of elimination, still mine.

I didn't go home after I left the house. I absconded in the late afternoon sun, down the fire road, ignoring the sting in my ankles from the plants I didn't care to avoid as I biked with pursed lips and watering eyes.

I wasn't sad, just deeply frustrated. The day wasn't what I had hoped, and I was utterly powerless to control it. That was, more than anything, an annoying feeling. I was fifteen, I didn't care for bigger feelings than that.

I hopped off my bike when I got to the trestle, but I didn't cross over it. I walked out to the middle, leaned my bike on the rail, and plopped down. It was quiet, save for the trickle of the creek. I preferred that calming sound over the gaudy din of the music at the party.

I sat there. I didn't yell or scream or throw things off the bridge or succumb to any sort of outburst of emotion at all. I just sat. And only then did I realize how tired I was. It had been a long day.

I noticed a box turtle walking over some rocks under me. Its dry shell of gray and speckles disguising it among the leaves and dirt and pebbles of the creek bed. It moseyed along, perhaps looking for some fresh vegetation to munch on. Perhaps simply walking to nowhere in particular.

I felt jealous of that little creature. It didn't know or care about high school interpersonal politics. I wished that I did, but my station in life didn't allow such pleasures.

"Enjoy it in this life while you can, dude," I said out loud and leaned my forehead into the midlevel support rail. I swung my legs in the air under me, under the trestle, like a little kid on a swing. The mountain air whooshing over my ankles, easing the sting of the cuts, and cooling my sweat-swollen feet was a glorious relief.

I was still sitting there when I heard footsteps on the bridge approaching. I looked back in the direction of the party to see a boy I only tangentially knew named Kevin Meade walking up and sitting down beside me.

"Some party, huh?" He exhaled at me.

"I guess you could say that."

Kevin was generally regarded as a "cool kid." A year older than me, tall, handsome. I didn't know any more than that about him. I had never had a conversation with him. I didn't know if he knew who I was. I would've liked to be able to say that I didn't care if he knew who I was, but I did. Everyone wants the cool kid to know their name—even if they don't want the cool kid to be their friend.

"Katie didn't partake in the drugs," he told me.

"How did you—"

"Saw your face, saw you leave," he said. "Put two and two together. You've got a pretty lousy poker face, by the way."

I laughed and then sighed. I looked out over the creek bed; I couldn't see the turtle anymore. The trees were taller than I had realized, still towering over us despite their bases being some twenty feet under us.

"What the heck does the phrase 'can't see the forest for the trees' mean?" Kevin asked.

I scoffed and looked at him with my mouth more open than I wanted it to be. I probably looked freshly lobotomized.

"Um, it means like, that someone is too focused on the details to see the big picture." I tried to explain.

"Yeah, that's what I thought," he said and tossed an oak leaf off the bridge, watching it drift down to its companions below. "Not sure what made me think of that."

He put his hand on my thigh, and I let him. He leaned in and kissed me. I had never kissed a boy before. I wanted to hate him because that totally was not a romantic moment, but I liked him—a high school superficial sort of like—and he wasn't doing coke.

We ended up dating for a while later that year. I lost my virginity to him. He was manipulative as hell, in hindsight. A lot of guys that age are, whether they realize it or not. It probably has something to do with how we raise boys, but I don't know. It could just be our nature as people.

Kevin finally left me for a prettier girl. He told me so—it's not just me being insecure. He taught me not to trust men on a first impression, and that was good in the long term, I guess, for as long as I was able to learn from it.

Nine

I rode with Theodore in his pickup truck from city hall. He promised he would bring me back to my car when we were done that night. I figured he would bring me back the next morning instead.

It was a pretty evening out, so we rode with the windows down. I'm sure my hair was all kinds of fucked up when I got out, but damn, it sure did feel good to enjoy the fresh air after a week stuck in the office. It was one of those mountain evenings when it was warm but without the sort of obtrusive humidity you'd get down toward the coast.

We pulled up to a building on the south side of town I had never been to before. It was an old warehouse, as far as I knew. For as long as I could remember, though, there was nothing in there. It was just one of the buildings you'd pass on the way out of town. I don't know why the city thought it would be a good idea to clear-cut a whole forest to build a giant warehouse, which, in short order, would serve no purpose at all—except for underground fighting. Money, I assume, considering some company paid a lot of money for the lot, and someone somewhere was presumably still paying taxes on the place.

"Don't look too hard at nobody," Theodore told me as we got out of the truck, and he met me around the front side of the hood. "You'll be liable to get challenged for a fight. And you can't say no to a fight."

"Have you ever been challenged?" I asked him, looking up to meet his eyes as we started walking. He was looking forward, checking out the cars that were already there and the few folks milling about. I wondered what he was looking for. Something, or someone, specific, I imagined.

"Once," he said, deadly fucking serious. I noticed his eyes darting around, jumpy almost. "It didn't go too well for me. I tended bar with an eye patch and a wad of gauze in my lip for a week. Can't recommend it." He looked at me and smiled, mock punching me in the shoulder. "And you got a real job, so don't get tempted now."

I smiled and chuckled nervously, charmed by Theodore but terrified of getting into a fight with someone who could throw a punch and mean it.

The inside of the warehouse resembled more of a high school gymnasium than it did a factory at that point. Metal folding chairs were set up around a foot-high raised platform, which seemed to be made from old pallets with plywood screwed on top—just like Theodore's "stage" at the bar. Maybe that's where he got the idea.

On one side, farthest from the entry, there was a small set of aluminum bleachers. Someone had stolen them from the actual high school, Theodore told me, my beloved alma mater. I wondered if they were stolen while I was there or sometime in the missing years between then and now.

The folding chairs were full, to my surprise. Maybe seventy-five people were there, but they made the space full enough. I recognized a few of the faces, vaguely. Folks I had gone to high school with, folks whom I saw around town, presumably, even some faces whom I had come across in my time with Mayor Wright's office—mostly because of trouble they had gotten into.

The rest, I assumed, were from neighboring towns. *Towns* being a relative term to mean that these people lived somewhere near Bellwether—near enough to drive over for an evening of illicit-adjacent activities. There weren't actually towns, so to speak, in that vicinity.

I thought I was poor. I thought I grew up working class. I thought I was tough. *These* were rough-and-tumble motherfuckers. These fuckers got beat by their parents and went to elementary school the next day and beat a classmate even worse. I heeded Theodore and tried to avoid looking anyone square in the eyes.

Theodore and I found a place to sit near the top of the aluminum bleachers. It wasn't comfortable. Then again, I don't imagine anything there was comfortable, nor was it meant to be. It was meant to get people in the mood to fight.

"First fight is always a cleanup," Theodore whispered to me once we sat down.

"What do you mean?"

"Normally the first fight is between two dudes who have no business scrapping with each other—someone almost always ends up in a stretcher, and it's almost always the same guy. He calls himself Gemstone. I think he likes the pain," he explained. "Then it's kind of every man for themselves. If you want to fight you walk up ringside and call next. The night always ends with a prize fight—the two biggest and drunkest dudes beat the sins out of each other for a bit until everyone loses their goddamned minds."

"What the hell is the prize?" I asked, blowing by him calling the pallets a "ring."

"Not getting killed, mostly," He chuckled and put his hand on the small of my back. I leaned over and gave him a kiss. He wasn't Kevin Meade. I actually liked Theodore. He didn't seem to want to use me, as much as I wasn't too blinded by my feelings to tell.

The first fight of the night started shortly after. A big guy with balding jet black hair, which he kept long and greased back. He was to fight—well, demolish—a little guy who indeed liked to be called Gemstone. Ironically, I recognized him from high school. His real name—or his name back then—was Mikey.

Mikey was maybe five-foot, with rough-cut blond hair and a wannabe beard.

Theodore told me Mikey was almost always in the first fight. Always challenged the biggest opponent he could. Always gave it everything he had. Always got absolutely cleaned up.

It was a short fight. Big Guy let Mikey get in a couple of cheap shots. Gloves down, straight to the chin. No power. Big Guy danced around a little, the wood thudding rhythmically under his feet. After he let Mikey have his fill, he shook out his arms like Ali taunting Michael Dokes, then unleashed a right hook. One punch and it was done. Mikey on the floor, out cold. That's how he expected it to go, I guess.

Two by two, we watched folks come up and slug the shit out of each other. Theodore stood up and cheered sometimes.

"Hit him! Hit him!" he bellowed. "Go southpaw! Uppercut! He's wobbling!"

Most of what he yelled seemed to be sort of tongue-in-cheek. I had never seen him get like that. He was really cutting loose. His jeans sagged down his butt a little each time he stood up, just to emphasize how skinny he was.

During one fight—apparently between two people whom Theodore knew, perhaps tangentially—he stood and was pumping his fists and letting 'em have it. I was worried he might put his foot in his mouth, so I put my hand on the small of his back and linked my pinky finger through his back belt loop. He reached back and held my hand, giving it a squeeze to tell me he knew what he was doing and that it was okay.

* * *

My father used to get into fights at bars. He wasn't a drunk for most of my childhood, exactly. But he drank on occasion. And on the occasions when he drank, he meant it.

My father was a hard personality to control when he was sober. It was a totally different story when he was six vodka tonics deep in a night of post-traumatic stress despair. And it only got worse as he aged and buried himself further into the bottle.

Most of the time he was smart enough to pick a fight with someone he could take—or at least someone he could spar with all right and wake up alive the next morning. He never explained the black eyes, nor did he ever apologize to Mom.

I didn't know until I was a little older. Sometime around middle school I started to hear the stories. It was Bellwether—someone always knew something, so everyone soon knew everything. I tried to ignore the stories as best I could. I didn't want to hear about the vile transgressions of my supposedly once-honorable father.

One time—and I can't confirm if this was true; all I know is what I was told—apparently, my father went out to a bar. A real dive. It's not there anymore and for good reason. The fire department eventually used it for practice. I'm not sure if crime went down in Bellwether afterward, but it was at least less centralized.

Anyway, my father went out, and one of our teachers from the middle school was there. I have no clue what Mr. Donahue was doing at the bar, or even if he really was there or if they were somewhere else. Middle school brains exaggerate and memories fade.

Mr. Donahue hadn't been drinking too much. He was tipsy, but that's no crime. He recognized my father and struck up a conversation. I don't know what he said, probably nothing, but my father tried to pick a fight.

Being a schoolteacher who had dealt with his fair share of fights, Mr. Donahue diffused the situation, and they never actually threw hands. He didn't say anything to me the next day, but he was looking at me different.

A classmate whose dad was also there, supposedly, told me what had happened. Their dad didn't keep secrets so well, I guess.

I wasn't sure what I wanted more after that day: my death or my father's. Either way, I'd have to wait a while.

I had moved out by the time I got my answer, and of course, it all started with my father being back at a bar on a Thursday night. I was living with Katie at that point, and as far as I knew, my father was no longer working. He had settled in nicely to the role of part-time drunk and full-time jackass. I'm not sure how he afforded alcohol. His government pension wasn't a lot, though I suppose he didn't have many expenses.

Anyway, it was in the spring of senior year when my father's mouth finally wrote a check his fists couldn't cash. I remember the heat. I can still feel my shirt sticking to my back on one of those impossibly hot March days that made you think winter had said its last goodbye. I was sitting on a too-hard wooden chair in Katie's kitchen when her mom came in and told me. She tried to hide the details from me, but I was older by then and stubborn as hell. I pressed and she obliged.

A long-haul trucker with a past was apparently sitting opposite my father at the bar. The blowhard who had besmirched my mother's goodness thought the trucker had looked at him wrong. Maybe he did, maybe he didn't. It shouldn't have mattered. My father shouted at him. Something belligerent. Something less witty than he thought it was, certainly.

The trucker told him to fuck off, but my father didn't listen. He was in the mood, he was drunk, and he demanded a fight. After enough verbal abuse, the trucker obliged. They took it outside, and the trucker let my father get in a couple of punches. They bounced off like nothing.

They probably felt like nothing. My father was weak from the early onset of an alcoholism that had to take him.

A couple of swift shots and my father hit the ground. Reports differ on what happened. Some say it was a boot. Some say rebar. Some say a tire iron. Who cares?

Blunt force trauma ended the life and dishonor of Lieutenant Strotherton. I was eighteen and parentless. Then again, I already had been for months.

* * *

Theodore didn't get challenged to a fight after all, even with his shouting. Thank God. Maybe people knew his deal. He never did seem to be worried about getting challenged. Maybe the soliloquy about fight challenges was simply a tall tale, something to entertain me.

At least I thought so, but then the next fight proved his story. Two guys sitting on opposite sides of the ring had been jawing, I thought playfully, for a couple of fights. After the fight between Theodore's maybe-friends, one of the guys stood up and walked across the ring.

Maybe five-seven, well-built, wavy and kempt brown hair. He could've been handsome but for the inferiority complex I could see from across the room.

A couple of words were exchanged, and the two men stood up and went at it. It was an entertaining fight. The other guy was taller but clearly not as strong. He tried his best to use his length to stay in the fight, but soon enough he got dropped. He didn't get knocked out fully, but the fight was over, he had lost. That seemed to be the rule that separated this from real boxing: if you hit the ground, you were done.

The two exchanged money and went back to their seats—tall guy looking a little bit wobbly. Theodore explained the bets on fights weren't uncommon but were generally a pretty bad reason to get into it with someone.

"Paying to get your ass kicked just don't seem too fun if you ask me," he said.

It struck me a touch odd that Theodore came to these fights but seemed to be quite a pacifist himself, though I'm sure he had been in fights in his life. I wondered if there was some ulterior motive—or maybe he just enjoyed watching people get beat up. A little sadistic if that were the case, but who was I to judge.

The last fight of the night was the best and the longest. Two mountains of men slugging it out. They went round and round, both of them landing blows that would have ended any of the previous fights. A heavyweight fight worthy of a finale ended when one of them took a stumble after a properly thunderous uppercut. It was exciting, but perhaps not my cup of tea.

Then it was time to leave, and as he stepped down the bleachers, Theodore took my hand—subtly, gently—and guided me through the crowd. Everyone had their fill, and the blood was beginning to dry on the plywood as folks made their way to the exit.

As we walked, I noticed a random guy loitering near the exit. His squared-off shoulders, twitchy hands, and wide stance betrayed his anticipation of something—or someone. He watched as we passed, giving me a predatory once-over, then he reached out and grabbed at my upper arm. I pulled away from him before he could get hold of me, which caught Theodore's attention. He quickly stepped between the man and me and gave him a *do not fuck with me* look. The predator-creep snorted a quick laugh and walked off. It was a true badass moment for Theodore who, earlier in the evening, had been schooling me on how to avoid getting into a fight. It also gave me a strange feeling in my gut from the back-to-back instants of fear then relief then love.

As we walked away, Theodore squeezed my hand a little tighter. I appreciated it. He got us out of the building quickly. If I didn't have him, I don't know how I would've gotten out—or if I would've even done it on my own two feet.

That's not to say I needed a man. I've never been about that patriarchal bullshit. I survived most of my life without reliance on my father. I survived my entire marriage without reliance on my husband—and all the years before I got married without no damn man to protect me.

I'm a tough woman, and I do always carry a knife, but I was outnumbered. I wasn't looking for a fight and neither was Theodore. A lot of the people in the room, I'm sure, were. Two is better than one, I guess.

We got back in Theodore's truck a little after nine o'clock. The event, as it were, had been just as sketchy as it had seemed when we left city hall. It had also turned out to be a legitimately good time.

I didn't love the fighting, exactly. Maybe it was the time with Theodore. Either way, I enjoyed myself more than enough for the night to have been worth it.

Once we were back in his truck, I mostly expected Theodore to ask me back to his place. Maybe ask me to the bar—or any bar. It was Friday night, after all. *Time to live it up*, I thought. Honestly, I also wanted him to ask me out. I felt some type of way toward him after he had taken care of me at the fights.

Maybe it was an exaggeration in my mind, and he didn't actually have to do anything. Maybe it was as simple as I was just that attracted to him. Maybe. But I wasn't yet convinced.

I was, however, convinced that he had done right by me—and he was an attractive man whom I had already spent a night with. I wanted another.

"Want to go grab a milkshake?" he asked as he started up the engine. I wasn't expecting that. It was much more wholesome than the thoughts running through my mind. But I did like the idea—I hadn't had a good milkshake in quite some time.

"Um, sure," I said, not sounding as easy about it as I felt inside.

"This guy runs a little shop, maybe twenty minutes out of town," he said with that damn smile growing. "He uses fresh milk, special stuff from special cows—or so he says—but good God, Jesse. I swear he must put something else in 'em too—best goddamn milkshake you'll ever taste."

"Well, okay then. Sounds like I'll have to be the judge of that." I stopped hiding my grin. "Let's do it."

By twenty minutes out of town, Theodore meant twenty minutes out of the other, far side of town. Twenty minutes to the north was Kennedy's Shake Shop. It was built into, no kidding, one-half of an old mobile home. Not a whole mobile home. Just half of one that looked, in the dim light, as if it had been quite literally chainsawed in half at some point.

Kennedy's was planted in the middle of an otherwise empty lot adjacent to a midsize lower-middle-class suburb—houses that were new enough to have not started falling apart yet, but will, inevitably.

Kennedy's was run by one man, ironically not named Kennedy. It was open when it was open and closed the rest of the time.

Kennedy's had two flavors: vanilla and vanilla with a cherry on top. To say it was reasonable that in all my years I had never heard of it would be an understatement. I was more amazed Theodore had even found it. *Hole-in-the-wall* didn't even begin to describe it.

As luck would have it, it was indeed open when we got there. Perhaps there was a bit more rhyme and reason to it than the sign out front made it seem. There were a couple of other cars parked out front. There was one window at which to order and pay—cash only. The rest of the lot was grass and gravel that people parked on, in as much of an order as they could without any semblance of lines or curbs.

I got out with Theodore and ill-looked-after gravel crunched under foot, echoing in the air as if amplified solely by the night. I followed a half step behind him to the window, looking up and about into the night, looking at Theodore, regarding the particular moment—a particularly strange and unexpected, but joyful nonetheless, moment of my life.

The sky was clear, and I could see more stars than usual. As much as Bellwether was not a city, it did have a modicum of light pollution. The air was cooler than it had been when we left the fight; night was setting in. By the clear light of the moon, I could make out the ridges of the higher peaks of the Appalachian Mountains distantly around us.

"Cherry or no cherry?" Theodore asked me as we reached the stand.

"Um, cherry, of course," I replied, nudging him playfully in the side.

"Damn right." He dosed his reply with southern charm. I had learned by this point that he could turn it on more when he wanted to. It was a tool, a conversational Swiss Army Knife, which he knew how to use expertly.

Once we got our milkshakes, we sat in Theodore's truck with the engine running and the radio softly playing a country station. There was a Guy Clark song I recognized playing. I didn't know the lyrics, though. It would've been fun to sing along, joke with Theodore, create conversation.

I didn't, though. The conversation was more or less nonexistent. We just sat in the quiet, eating for a bit. I hummed and *mm-mm*ed to signal that the milkshake was as good as advertised. It was, for what it's worth, a really good milkshake. I hadn't come for the milkshake, though.

"You know, I didn't used to go to the fights." Theodore shattered the quiet.

"No?" I asked. I got the sense he was going to continue whether I said anything in response or not. I helped him along.

Theodore swirled his milkshake around with a straw and pursed his lips. I couldn't tell if he had changed his mind and was done talking or was looking for the right words. In the light of the dashboard, I could see something in his eyes. I couldn't identify the feeling, but it was strong. I waited for him to make the move.

"Nah," he said without much conviction and pursed his lips again before he continued. "My ex-wife didn't like me to go. She thought it was a rough crowd and, honestly, you know, she ain't wrong."

"Do you enjoy going?" I asked him. It was loaded; I knew it.

He smiled ironically and looked over at me.

"Not even really that much," he said. "It's fun, no doubt, but I mostly enjoy it because Mary didn't let me."

I mouthed *Mary* to myself. I didn't know her name before then.

"It's sort of healing, I suppose," he continued. "Maybe it's helping me move on. Maybe it isn't. I sure enjoyed going with you tonight more than I've ever enjoyed it before."

Theodore paused again, and I finally figured out what he was *really* talking about.

"You loved her, didn't you?"

"Yeah, I really did," He sort of grimaced and looked out the window, away from me. "But, hell, now I don't know."

"Yeah," I said softly. I observed his silhouette, turned away from me out the window. "Yeah . . . Well, I never really loved my husband, I guess, but it still hurt when he left. I mean, that's how I met you. I was at the bar because I was so sad over it. I don't normally drink that much. Ironic as it sounds, he didn't like the bar when we were together, and I went that night because of it. I wanted to go because he didn't. Similar to you, I guess.

"I loved being married, I think, but at the end of the day, Jeff and I were just so different. Our marriage didn't make enough sense. It made more sense when he left. It should've been a surprise that it took him so long."

Theodore stayed facing out of the window for a while longer. He deadpanned at the people across the parking lot, and I couldn't tell if I had shared too much. But then he turned to me.

"That's interesting," he said, completely earnestly, in a different tone that betrayed he had been truly thinking something over.

"What is?" I couldn't quite understand where his mind had gone; I didn't follow.

"That we had such different marriages, but at the end of the day, our spouses both left, and we both have been struggling in sort of the same way." He tried on a smile.

"Grief works in interesting ways," I offered. I was unexpectedly proud of the line.

"I'll drink to that." He raised his glass and took a big draw of his milkshake. I laughed and he did, too. The setting was comically different from the bar, and I loved that. I couldn't help but smile. I smiled more when he leaned over and kissed me.

"So what is the deal exactly with the fights?" I tried to change the subject, to grant him some normalcy after the deeper moment. "Like, how did they start?"

"I don't know really," Theodore answered. "I suppose folks wanted a way to blow off steam, and enough of 'em wanted to have some sort of fight club, and it went from there. But I don't know for sure."

"Why do they have it at the warehouse, though?" I was curious. "Was there not a way to have it in a little less of a sketchy way?"

"Oh, hell no, and ain't no one wanted to be the one to look into making it legal," he said emphatically. "It's always the guy who tries to do things the right way who gets in trouble. Plus, some friend of a friend of a friend, I think, is the one who owns the building these days. It's just easier this way."

"Huh, I guess that makes sense."

Theodore nodded and took another sip of his milkshake.

"See, when you make something illegal, something folks really—I mean *really* want to do—stuff they're gonna do, anyway, they've just got to go three floors underground to do it," Theodore explained.

"Three floors underground?" I asked.

"It's something my mama said one time. Always stuck with me," he continued. "When you're doing something illegal, you've got to do it underground. But when you're doing something *real* illegal, you've got to go even further underground. You've got to feel sure you aren't getting caught. You're gonna do it, anyway—but the deeper you go, the less likely you are to get caught."

"Three floors underground," I repeated. I thought about my conversation with Mayor Wright. I thought about life at large. I thought about how Theodore and I had to take different paths and, for some reason, ended up at the same place and how no matter how far underground you go, there's always a path back to the surface.

Ten

Katie and I didn't go to the house for a while after the party. Other people may have. Hell, Katie may have. I don't know. It's not like we talked about it. I wasn't exactly mad at Katie, just frustrated. But I think she knew that.

No, she was my best friend; she knew that, too. She tacitly understood I wasn't interested in going back to the house after that experience. Not yet, anyway. And she knew why. That was the best thing about Katie in our childhood: we could disagree, we could not speak for a couple of days, but we were fine. Eventually, we would be fine. That's how friendship should be, I thought.

We were hanging out one day during fall break of sophomore year, and we were at Katie's house, only fifteen months before it also became my house. I'm not sure why we needed a fall break, Thanksgiving break would come soon enough. One of the idiosyncrasies of the schooling that we all sort of accepted without questioning it.

It was a weekday, so her dad was out of town, and her mom was piddling around the house. We were lying on the floor talking, watching MTV. By this time, MTV had switched from being music television to a purveyor of reality garbage dealing with people whose lives were wholly different from mine. It didn't have my attention, suffice to say.

It was a rainy day. The first real cool, rainy day of fall. October in Bellwether, you never know what you'll get. Well, back then at least, before the climate crisis took proper hold. Back then, we would get those haunting days, maybe even a rare week, of inauspicious hot summer air, but we also got sweet whispers of fall. Cold fronts. Rainstorms that lasted for days. Crispness in the air, gentle against the skin. Relief from suffocating humidity. Those first few signs that we did still live in the mountains, not down in the gaudy piedmont somewhere.

This was one of those days. It was the first day of the year when you could get away with turning off the ceiling fan. I didn't. I needed that moving air, and I liked it cooler. The ceiling fan stayed on year around—I didn't care how much snow was on the crowd, no one could tell me otherwise. Besides, not everyone up in the mountains had air conditioning—in fact, most people in Bellwether didn't. In buildings such as those, typically older houses, a ceiling fan was a gift from God.

"Want to go up to the house?" Katie whispered toward me.

I thought for a minute. I didn't feel disagreeable, and I was happy with my friend, for the moment. I was in.

"Yeah, sure," I replied. "Will your mom be okay with it?"

"Let's find out." Katie tried a wink at me. Katie could *not* wink. But for someone who couldn't wink, she winked a lot. She loved scrunching the right side of her face up into what could be interpreted as a wink. "Hey, Mom! Is it okay if Jesse and I go biking?"

Katie's mom was in the kitchen, baking a pie with fruits and berries they had grown themselves. A grateful teen would have helped her bake in hopes of getting a piece. I was not a grateful teen. If only nostalgic wishing made it so.

She stopped what she was doing and sighed lightly when Katie asked. She pursed her lips, slightly to the right, and gave the simmering pot one more stir. She was generally a happy woman, but she was also a good mom who could infer when her child was up to no good. She also loved Katie with every bit of her soul.

"Um, okay," she said. "Just be home before supper."

Supper was, even then, a bit of an old-fashioned word. It made me roll my eyes, but also smile. It was quaint, in a pleasing way. That's how Katie's mom was, generally.

Katie agreed, smiling excitedly at her mom who had turned her back. It was the smile of the rookie outfielder who is sure he has the hall of fame pitcher figured out, right before he gets struck out swinging and falls on his ass. As smart as Katie was, or I was, our moms had been around longer. They were smarter, but they didn't let us know it.

We were suited up in our rain jackets—not enough—and our far-too-porous bike helmets. We were both wearing blue jeans and some variety of Chuck Taylor wannabes.

It was *pouring*. It was like God had decided to end the farm's growing season in one fell swoop and send the deer and bears—and gullible humans—running for an ark in the hills that was never coming.

It should not have been news to us that blue jeans do not dry quickly when wet, and by the time we made it to the house, we were both well and truly soaked. Not only that, but we also had both become gaudily painted with red clay and pine decay mud from bike tires ripping through runoff ruts.

It was loud in the house. Not like from the party. A constant white noise, too loud to be in the background, too quiet not to be calming. The rain pounded the roof, and I worried it wouldn't hold. It was an old house; it had been there for years, weathering hundreds of storms worse than this one. Of course it was going to hold. Though, I suppose, there is a moment in the life of everything that's ever collapsed, just before it fell, when it too had weathered everything it faced and held strong.

The dryness inside was a relief, I suppose, but I didn't feel dry. I walked around, contemplating, when I caught Katie stripping down out of the corner of my eye.

"What?" She shrugged at me, catching my gaze.

"Nothing." I laughed at the scene, turning to see my now half-nude best friend. Katie laughed, too, and hung up her jeans and jacket on the remnants of Jimi's table. I hesitated then followed suit and hung up my jeans. I didn't hang up my jacket; instead I lay it on the ground to sit on.

Katie sat down beside me, putting her bare butt on the not-clean—and not-exactly intact—floor. I tried not to be grossed out.

We sat there together, admiring our escape. Katie wore a prideful grin, the corners of her mouth doing nothing to hide the fact that she felt like she was doing something the world didn't want her to. Katie liked that feeling, if it was not yet obvious.

I looked out of the window at the rain. It hadn't slowed down a bit. The trees whispered their relief, some of them relinquishing, for the first time in the season, their browning leaves.

"So," I said into the space after a while, expecting Katie to have had a reason for coming up here. She did, in her mind, I guess.

"So . . ." She tried to start but trailed off. She looked away from me, then back into the liminal space between us. I gave her that space alone and turned to the window. "I felt bad about the party, I think. I didn't realize it would get so out of hand."

I could tell she had put real thought into what she wanted to say. That didn't make it easier. *I think* is not a qualifier to an apology that imbues confidence. It meant something to me, though. My friend knew me well enough to recognize it wasn't all okay.

I let her words hang in the air for a beat.

"Yeah." I started. "It wasn't really you, I guess. I just wasn't expecting the drugs, and you seemed into it. I was worried, mostly, you would partake."

"I didn't." She hid her defensiveness well.

"I'm glad." I endeavored to smile. "I was surprised, mostly. But it wasn't fair for me to hold a grudge over it. You weren't the one who pushed the party to that point. You were just having fun."

"I was." She let me spin myself into a web.

"There's nothing wrong with that." I kept running. "I don't even know the guy who brought out the cocaine . . ."

"Rick." Katie clarified. "He's a decent guy. He asked me on a date at one point. I said no."

"Didn't seem that decent to me." I pushed back.

"People do drugs, Jess," she said sharply, defensively. "I try not to judge people on the worst thing they do. If doing coke is the worst thing Rick does, I can live with it, y'know. I'm sure folks did worse things that day—maybe not here." She gestured to the house around us. "But maybe after."

"Yeah, you're probably right." I didn't think Katie was right. I still didn't like people doing drugs. Fear, I guess. Fear is a powerful thing. By that point in my life, I had been alive long enough to see people ruined by drugs. My worldview would be solidified in that matter not long after by Marianne's death. Even if her death didn't affect me too much personally—though it did, in reality—it reinforced my view that sure, yes, people did drugs, whatever, but I didn't want drugs to be a part of my life.

Katie and I sat there for a while after, chatting about school and boys, my budding and doomed romance with Kevin who would soon try, but fail, to break my heart—I had bigger issues coming, harder days coming. I sat in the childhood-like reverie of my afternoon with Katie. It was the first one we had enjoyed in a long while, and it mended our friendship. A friendship that would only be strengthened, then shattered, by the year and a half of trials that followed.

We didn't know what doom lurked then, and we didn't care.

The rain never subsided that day. It came down hard then continued for days after. The cold sank in as winter tempted us with its coming presence. In my family,

I suppose, after Marianne died that December, winter never truly left.

Eleven

After our night at the fight, Theodore and I exchanged numbers. It was a realization of the obliviating of uncertainty, which I liked. He also still had a flip phone. It was humble and earnest and fit him well. I liked that, too.

He was punching my number into his phone and finally asked me the question everyone gets to eventually. He entered my name, *J-e-s-s-i-e*, and I corrected him. "No *I*."

"Really?" he asked, smirking at me. "I never met a girl Jesse spelled like that."

"Yeah, well, there aren't really any others."

"Then how did you end up with your name spelled that way?"

"My father wanted a boy," I told him. "He was pretty pissed when I came out. No dick. Still decided to name me the way he'd planned on. Mom didn't have any say in it. She didn't have a say in shit in our house."

"Tough break, but I like it," Theodore said, then kissed me goodnight.

I was glad Theodore had a way to get in touch with me besides coming into the office or hoping I came by the bar. I wondered if it would be another week-plus before he asked me out again. I hoped he wouldn't wait that long, I wanted to see him again. Thankfully, he didn't wait long.

That very Saturday morning, just hours after our date the night before, before I had even had my morning coffee, my phone buzzed. He didn't wait for me to say anything when I picked up.

"You ever seen a shooting star?" I could hear that grin from the other end of the line.

"I can't say I have," I lied, probably. He had put a smile on my face. I knew he had something in mind, and I wanted to hear what it was.

"Clear sky up there on the mountain tonight," he said. "I bet I can show you one. Got to go up on the hill, though, but I know a place."

By "know a place," Theodore meant he had a friend of a friend of a guy at the bar who owned a farm whom Theodore had gotten to know. He had talked the farmer's ear off one night.

They gave him permission to go up and park by their pasture at night to stargaze—a deal he made for the express purpose of that date. They also gave him permission to fish in their pond, which was exciting to Theodore because they kept it stocked with largemouth bass, but I didn't care as much about that. It was true to his character to pull off that bit of dealmaking through charm, though. Say what you will about Theodore, you can't accuse him of not being personable.

"I'm game."

"Pick you up around ten?" he asked rhetorically. "I recommend stealing a wink this afternoon." He chuckled.

"Okay, sounds good." I returned the laugh. "See you tonight."

Despite Theodore's advice, I didn't take a nap that afternoon. I tried. I tossed and turned for over an hour, but anticipation is the enemy of rest. I gave up after a while and watched TV. I watched TV while pacing back and forth like a madwoman, striding anxiously between my living room and bedroom debating what to wear.

Should I dress nice? Casual? I can't wear sweats, can I? We're going late at night. It's cool out, but not cold, so no coat, just a light jacket. What is Theodore going to think I look good in, and do I care?

Just *that*, for hours. I made myself eat dinner around seven, but I ate standing up at my kitchen counter, then resumed pacing. My legs were tired, honestly, by the time the sun set. I couldn't even put a finger on why I was so in the throes of anticipation, but I was. It was an unusual experience and an unusual emotion for me. I didn't mind it, though. New, in that case, was good. There weren't any surprises, no last minute plans or things to be anxious or anticipatory about in my marriage to Jeff.

As it is wont to do, night did eventually fall. One thing I've found you can count on in life is that, whether you want it to or not, time will keep moving. And, as promised, Theodore pulled up in front of the house at just after ten o'clock. He got out to greet me—to come knock on my door and pick me up like the proper gentleman some sort of chivalrous instinct told him to be—but he didn't need to. His boots had barely hit the ground outside of his truck door, and I was already out with the door locked behind me.

"Howdy stranger" was his go-to opener. It struck me as ironic that the word *stranger* was anything but descriptive of reality—it made me wonder if that was how he greeted everyone. I tried to remember if I'd ever seen him greet someone besides me, but I couldn't. I let myself believe it was a phrase all my own, though I knew it probably wasn't.

"Not bad on the punctuality," I joked. I gave him a peck on the lips when he walked over to the passenger side and opened the door for me.

"Can't be late for important things." He smiled then chuckled before he could get the punchline out. "Work? Now that I can be late for. If only the ole boss saw it the same way."

"Tell me about it," I said, even though I couldn't really relate. I had never been late to a day of work, even on my darker days.

"So where is this farm?" I asked once we were already a few miles down the road and not nearly anything close to what Theodore had described.

"If you go up to past Kennedy's and take a right up the hill, just keep going for like ten miles, and there's a little gravel driveway up top, and it opens up into open pasture. It's hard to find, but once you're there, it's pretty damn hard to miss."

"Does Percy live up there?"

"During busy season, yeah, but he's also got a place in town where he lives with the family most of the time in the winter when nothing will grow," Theodore explained. "He's actually kind of loaded. I don't even think he needs to run the farm anymore to be set for life. Nice as can be, though. He really is."

And so it was, we took the right up the hill, and ten minutes later, we turned into what seemed to be nothing. It did, as Theodore had explained, turn into a gravel driveway. Theodore drove to the end, to where the road was nowhere to be seen, and the sky was endless.

We got out of the truck after he put it in park. Well, I did. Theodore turned around to behind his seat and pulled up an honest-to-God wicker basket. I wanted to ask him where he got it. Did he buy it? I couldn't imagine a guy like Theodore going to the store and buying a wicker basket—which is normative bullshit, in hindsight. But maybe he inherited it; maybe it was a relic of his still-looming divorce.

I didn't ask. I was charmed by the fact that from the wicker basket, on the tailgate around back, Theodore pulled out a blanket, two glasses, a bottle of wine, and a bag of cheese puffs. The wine wasn't expensive, but it was wine, and it wasn't like I could taste the difference—I was no sommelier—and the glasses were real glasses, not plastic. I raised an eyebrow at the cheese puffs, though. Theodore clocked my look.

"Well, I figured cheese goes with wine, but I wasn't sure if cheese would travel well out here what with the lack of refrigeration," he explained, then gestured at the bag. "So next best thing. If cheese puffs ain't fine dining, I don't think I care to know what is."

The explanation made me laugh. It was so preposterous—the whole situation was, really—but I totally understood his thought process. I'm not sure what that said about our relationship at that point. But it also so happened that I liked cheese puffs enough, so I couldn't be mad, anyway.

I helped him lay out the blanket in the bed of his truck, and he helped me climb on. I sat with my back against the cab and watched him climb up behind me. A sign of the quality of the wine: it had a metal twist top in lieu of a cork. Industrious—and a good thing because surely Theodore did not have a corkscrew with him.

He poured us each a strong pour and sat down beside me. It was almost eleven o'clock, and the sky had turned to a deep dark. I felt Theodore exhale beside me, settling into the blanket beneath us after a long day.

"And now . . ." He dragged out his sentence. "We wait."

He turned and smiled at me. I smiled back and raised my glass to cheers it against his.

I watched him take the first sip to see if the wine we were to be imbibing was palatable, but his poker face was too good. I took a sip. The wine was worse than Theodore's poker face. *Oh well*, I thought. Theodore opened the bag of cheese puffs, a bit hastily, to signal that he agreed with me about the wine.

I let the silence hold for a while—trading crunches of our snack and crinkles of the bag to fill the noise gap in the silent night. We looked at the sky, hoping for a sign of something moving out there. After a while of seeing nothing, I turned to look at Theodore. There was a look of glowing wonder in the reflection of the pleasant starlight in his eyes. I watched him watch the night for a while then turned back to turn our joint gaze onto the stars above, succumbing to the wonder of a mutual appreciation of the third thing.

"So how did you come up with this idea?" I asked without moving my gaze from where it was out toward the depths of the observable universe.

"Well, I had gotten the idea a while back. Got the permission to come out here," he explained. "But then, not gon' lie to you, I kind of forgot about it. Then last night I thought I might've seen a shooting star. I thought that was pretty damn cool, and it made me get to itching to see more. Called Percy up this morning to make sure it was cool, then I called you."

I didn't know what to say that didn't feel too cheesy, so I just smiled.

He leaned in and kissed me, reading my eyes to find that what I wanted to say couldn't be said with words. I had to accept that, ready or not, I liked him—at least more than I had liked anyone since before Jeff. I'm not sure I ever really liked Jeff—at least not in such an honest way, an easy way. The feelings were real with Theodore, and I knew it.

We slept there that night in the bed of his truck. We saw shooting stars, sure, but that wasn't the point. The point was this: with shared togetherness despite our troubles, there can be peace and contentedness and even hope in the world still. Despite it all, even if only for a moment, even we could appreciate being alive, and we could appreciate it together.

The sun rose early in the morning, over the hill in the distance—somewhere far off in the east. It illuminated before us the vast pasture and the speckled marks of cows below, grazing down in the valley.

Theodore was already awake when I opened my eyes. He was holding my hand, lying on his back, looking up into the brightening sky. I almost didn't want to let him know I was up, he looked so at peace. He felt me move my hand, though, and turned and smiled at me.

He leaned over and kissed me, and his morning breath wasn't as bad as I expected. I felt ashamed because I probably smelled. But then again, he probably did, too. We probably smelled like each other, I guess.

We lay with each other for a while, waking up slowly with the day. Somewhere in the distance a rooster woke up and crowed, ironically, comfortably after us. We watched the cows move together, almost as a single mass, across the pasture. There was a small creek that fed a relatively even smaller pond down the hill. Cows can swim, or so Katie told me when we were kids. I didn't know. I had never seen it done. Maybe that's where the cows were going. Good for them. Everyone should have a morning as happy as one spent swimming in an Appalachian Mountain pond with clear and crisp water.

I felt a headache awakening in my head as I did. Probably from the wine. Or the lack of water. Or both. But it wasn't bad enough for me to care, so I didn't.

"Want to grab some breakfast?" Theodore asked. It was light enough that I was beginning to feel the faint heat of the rising sun on my cheeks. "Coffee would probably do us some good."

"Yeah." I smiled. "Coffee sounds great."

"There's a gas station down the other side of the hill a ways. They've got a little grill," he said. "It's mostly truckers 'cause it feeds in from the highway, but it's pretty damn good—good bacon."

"Crispy?"

"Damn crispy."

"I do like a good piece of crispy bacon."

"Then we better get a move on." He gave me another kiss, which I held for longer, then packed up his basket.

After breakfast, which did include, as promised, excellent bacon, Theodore and I walked out into the parking lot. The light of midmorning, the sun having risen fully above the hills, was bright and made me squint my eyes.

On the way to his truck, we had to pass a row of 18-wheelers. As we passed, I took my hand from his and reached out to write in the dust on the back of one, in big block letters: JESSE + THEODORE. I wasn't sure why I did it. It was a bit childish, but I gave into the compulsion, anyway. It felt, I guess, happy.

"Not bad." He smiled and stepped over to me and the dirty metal canvas we had before us. He reached with one pointer finger— reminiscent of E.T.—and touched the metal. He looked at the tip of his index finger then rubbed it together with his thumb, examining the qualities of the dust. I chuckled. I thought it looked like he had never seen or touched a truck or dirt before.

Then to my surprise, he reached back out and in gorgeous script wrote out: Theodore & Jesse with dramatic and elegant capital *T* and capital *J*. A calligrapher at work.

"Woah, now." I stepped back. "Where'd you learn to do that, Mr. Unabomber?"

He laughed then looked down and rubbed his chin. It seemed like he wasn't sure if he wanted to tell me the truth, so I just waited for him to decide. He would say something, whether it was the full story or not, and I wanted him to know it was his decision what he would say.

"Me and my boys. We used to write and draw on the backs of trucks like this all the time. We had five of us. We were a gang, really, I guess is what you would call it. Called ourselves the 'Bellwether Boys.'" He smiled. "Would do anything for each other. They had my back, I had theirs. We'd fuck someone up if you messed with one of the Boys. Anyway, we'd compete to see who could make the best art—I got to know what kind of dust was best for it, too. This one here is all right. Not great but it works."

I had never heard Theodore talk much about his friends. It seemed like such an important part of his youth. I was surprised he'd never mentioned it.

"Do you still see any of those guys?" I asked. He paused and thought again. I could see in his eyes that I'd hit a nerve.

"Nah . . ." He started, then trailed off again. "I had to stop hanging out with them."

He stopped. I probably could have just let it go, but I didn't. I wanted to know more. I wanted to know everything about him. The sunlight stole between the truck and the one adjacent and lit his face a bright gold. He looked handsome, but there was some sort of feeling in his face, but I couldn't make it.

"Oh, why?" I asked.

"Well, it started with just trespassing," he said. "We'd go mess around at old buildings. Then we'd try to sneak into places after they closed. Big stores mostly. I didn't see so much harm in it, but it was illegal, y'know. It was fun, though. We'd sneak in and just sort of walk around. It was the thrill of being somewhere we weren't supposed to, I think.

"Anyway, then some of the guys decided to start taking stuff from the stores. I turned a blind eye to it for a while, but I disagreed with what they were doing, to be honest. I just wanted to go in and hang out. I had no interest in stealing other folks' stuff. Just seemed wrong to me.

"Well, then the Boys started wanting to try to rob places. I went with 'em for a while. We'd go hold up a gas station, get some beers and maybe fifty bucks from the register, y'know. Nothing too crazy but my boys got a real kick out of it, and they were my friends, so I didn't say nothing.

"The problem came when they just kept on wanting to go bigger and bigger and bigger." His accent thickened as he talked. I could tell he meant what he was saying. He felt the pain of what he was saying. "Well, and you know how the nineties were, drugs were running crazy. The Boys realized they could spend the money they stole to buy drugs. Then they realized that they could rob a damn drug store and sell the drugs themselves and make even more money. It was a whole goddamn mess.

"I stopped hanging with them after the first time they robbed a convenience store to get drug money. Cops showed up at my folks' place asking questions on me. I couldn't handle it. Told the truth to 'em. They let me off easy, but a couple of the Boys caught charges and had to do some community service. We couldn't look at each other straight after that . . ." He looked up at his calligraphy—our names together. "Last I heard, three of 'em were in prison. Drugs, goddamn. 'Round here they'll get you—sooner or later those sons of bitches will get you.

"The other, Willie, died in a freak accident—must've been near fifteen years ago now. Fell off his bike on a trail and hit his head weird. Game warden found him. I can still hear his mama's cries at the funeral."

The silence after he finished was thick. It hovered in the air between us and obscured his eyes from my view. There were, and are, no words to say in a moment like that. I reached out and grabbed his right hand with my left and twirled with my thumb.

"Okay." I spoke as softly as my voice would let me.

Twelve

Most people, no matter where—Bellwether, Brooklyn, Bel Air, it doesn't matter, want their sixteenth birthday to be special. They want it to be the best day of their life so far. That's the way it's supposed to be, right? Sweet sixteen is what we hear, what we've been fed by popular culture.

Mine was not.

Mine was December fourth, the day after Marianne died. Not long before the Christmas holiday. I was almost done with school for the term.

There was always a great feeling in the air that time of year. Even teachers sort of let you check out. Everyone was talking about their plans. What they wanted for Christmas, where they wanted to go, what they wanted to do. Most of us knew well that it was just that: dreaming. But we dreamed, anyway, and the air smelled sweet and cold.

There was snow on the ground that year, I remember that. Not a lot, it wasn't even too cold, it was just pleasant. The town, despite its downfalls, was always decorated real pretty for the holiday season. I did like that a lot about Bellwether.

Having my birthday fall that time of the year always made it even more special. Mostly at school. Mostly with Katie. There, folks gave me the attention I needed but didn't really want yet.

Not that my folks didn't do anything. I have to admit, even my father did everything he could to make my birthday special most years. It didn't do much to ease the tensions in the house, but looking back, I appreciated that. Mom, of course, couldn't do a ton, but did a ton with what she could.

That year, though, in the darkened winter of 2004, no one was going to make my birthday special that year. It was anything—*anything* but joyous, anything but merry.

Mom's screams will never be fully extricated from my mind. They sting, far within my soul, like a bad tattoo with needles piercing too deep. The scars remain, without any form of redemption—no beautiful flower or swooping bird to hide the place where the puncture in my soul was made.

Marianne didn't have much family out of town. Everyone she was related to—anyone she had ever loved or was loved by was in or damn close to Bellwether. No one in Bellwether can afford to house a body for two weeks to let whomever from wherever get to town. Funerals happened quick here—no long planning process or elegant visitations at the local funeral parlor.

Bury the body; that was the cheap way, the expedient way, the only way.

Marianne died on the third. They put her casket in the ground on the fifth. The snow had started melting; deep soil was still warm from the dissipating fall. The earth seemed to accept its lost child back in, despite the cries of Mom hoping to stop it.

It was silent in the mountains that day, actually. It was almost eerie. At funerals, there isn't ever much noise, anyway, but it was as if the whole region had come to a halt.

I remember the broken clouds in the sky and the look they gave the pine trees lining the graveyard. They looked darker, more ominous than usual—like they were trying to tell me something was coming.

It was so silent. So quiet that Mom's wails echoed through the hills. But cries are never constant. Lungs demand air in between the heinous screams, and in that break, there was silence. I will never forget that silence, broken only by a distant songbird, wailing a cry of its own from one of those pine trees. Later in my life I read Kurt Vonnegut and remembered that day enough that I had to close the book. I remembered that bird and how it made me feel about Mom and loss and grief and that awful cycle everyone in Bellwether seemed to be in.

Poo-tee-weet. It wasn't a question in my story, it was a warning.

The next Saturday, I went over to Katie's. That wasn't abnormal, but when I walked in, her mom took me into the kitchen and showed me a big cake. It was homemade, one of her many excellent pieces of baking, made with love in their too-small kitchen, without help from Katie or Katie's dad.

In shaky, but legible writing—thoughtfully done, tediously done, to the best of her ability—the cake said: *Happy Sweet 16, Jesse!*

I'd thought everyone had forgotten. No one had said happy birthday to me on my actual birthday, nor the day after, nor the day after that.

Mom, without malice, and for good reason, probably simply forgot. My father did, too, though I can't say in good faith that it wasn't intentional that year with Marianne's death and all.

I hadn't been to school on account of the funeral arrangements, so there was no one to say anything there. No well-meaning teacher to whisper a kind aside or random acquaintance who happened to know. Not to mention, I hadn't even seen Katie aside from very briefly in the receiving line at the service.

It had been, more than ever before, as if my birthday simply hadn't happened.

Katie's mom didn't forget. She and Katie, and Katie's dad who was home at the time, sang happy birthday to me as if everything was all well and good. I hadn't cried since the funeral, even in my saddest moments, but son of a bitch if that family getting together and singing for me didn't make me sob like a child who'd lost their parent in the store.

It was all pent-up emotions. I had held all of my anger, and angst, and sadness, and raw pain in for a while. It just had to come out sometime. Holding that shit in for too long will kill you dead—stress isn't beneficial for health as it turns out.

Still, it didn't happen again for a long time. I didn't let it out, didn't let myself *feel* in that way again until Mom died. Vulnerability was never my strong suit.

* * *

After Mom died, I had a decision to make. It had been a hard year since Marianne died, which made sense. But still, Mom had sort of held together a façade, and that at least had made life bearable for me. If she had gone then, I think I probably would have gone with her.

My father was still a piece of shit, but what was new. That short period of him pretending to be a caring husband after Marianne died ended abruptly come January. I wish I was surprised, but I wasn't. A piece of shit abuser is going to be a piece of shit abuser.

I remember distinctly the night his outlying behavior reverted back to its lousy mean. Mom had cooked dinner, as she always did—despite, mind you, being in the throes of the most abject kind of grief imaginable. But she had cooked; I think it was meatloaf? It was some sort of meat dish, I know that. She had cooked it just a little bit off. I think, honestly, he was just looking for an excuse to blow off some steam. As much as I struggled to let out any emotion, my father struggled to keep his rage in. He was bursting at the seams from not even a month of holding it in.

I sat on my bed and turned on my radio. I put it on quietly. That way I had something to listen to other than my father yelling, but it wasn't loud enough for him to turn that anger onto me for disturbing him in some minute way.

Maybe I should have. Maybe I should have taken one for the team—stepped between him and Mom and defended her. Maybe I should have turned the radio on full blast just that once and let him break through the wood of my bedroom door like an abominable Kool-Aid Man and wail on me instead that time. But I didn't. I didn't think to. I wish I had.

It's not like I hadn't before. I was a loudmouth at times growing up. I got into trouble plenty. I got yelled at and whooped more times than I'd care to admit for things I said—sassy remarks and even sometimes defenses of Mom. I didn't that night, though. I had calmed a bit maybe, not as willing to stick my head in the lion's mouth just to get in the last word or make a witty remark.

Anyway, we lasted a year like that until the day he went too far. I knew I couldn't live with my father. I knew the abuse would be mine and mine alone. I could take it when it was divided between Mom and me, but just me, I think my fate would have been the same as hers—and much quicker. I wasn't as strong as she was; I couldn't take that abuse for that long, and I didn't have a daughter I loved more than myself to protect.

Moving to Katie's house seemed logical. Her parents were okay with it, too. I don't think her dad really cared, to be honest, and her mom wasn't going to put me out. She was such a caring lady, she even set me up with my own mattress in Katie's room. It was a twin mattress on the floor, but to me it was a memory foam California king. Sure, it was hard at first, but after a period of adjustment, I felt like I was staying at the Four Seasons, and for the first time in my life, the evenings were quiet, almost peaceful.

I saw my father from time to time, but I mostly tried to avoid him. He was around town, and the town was still small. I think he also wanted to feel some kind of ownership of me. He wanted me to move back in with him, but I figured it was only because he felt like he was supposed to want me to.

He was still my father, but that doesn't mean anything when he doesn't treat you like a daughter.

* * *

Theodore and I kept seeing each other regularly after our night at the farm. We went to supper a couple nights a week. I visited him at the bar when I could—politely sitting through a few more of his music performances. He even brought me lunch to work once. We were, as it were, *dating*.

So when Mayor Wright told me we were having a big banquet to honor a retiring city council member and that I had a plus-one, it made sense to bring Theodore. We weren't in a defined relationship. We hadn't talked about what we were or what we were doing. Most of the folks at work had met him, but folks were generally respectful enough not to ask. There's an energy undefined couples have that isn't hard to recognize—like seeing a solo bear cub in the woods. You want to find out where the mama is, the cub may need her. But it's best to quietly back away and stay clear of danger. Though, in reality, most bear attacks are by lone male bears. I think there's an analogy there; you do the math.

Still, unless I brought it up—which I hardly, if ever, did—the folks I worked with would never say anything. It was a workplace, so it was professional unless someone made a concerted effort to make it friendly.

Christina, whom I interacted with the most, was always the consummate professional, and honestly, Bill was the only one from work with whom I had that close of a relationship. But he and I hadn't talked about it. Not that

I was avoiding it, exactly. I just didn't know what to say even if I did want to talk about it. And even without them asking about it, I knew I felt something changing in me. Sort of like skydiving for the first time, but I wasn't sure if I had a parachute.

"Teddy!" I almost shouted when he picked up the phone. I had found out he hates being called Teddy, so naturally I had to beat him over the head with it sometimes. "You own a suit?"

"Damn right." He didn't miss a beat. "Who the hell doesn't own a suit? My daddy would come back from the grave to holler at me if I didn't own a black suit. Can't show up to a funeral in anything less."

"Good." I decided to poke at him a bit more. "Can you behave yourself at a formal gathering of our most esteemed local government officials?"

"No promises." He played along with a chuckle. "Might stage a coup—can never really be sure."

"Well if something comes up and you need to stage a coup, just know I'm not bailing you out."

"Well that's only fair given your profession I'd say."

"Good," I said. "I'll pick you up around six?"

"I'll be ready, and I'll even let you straighten my tie."

The banquet was on a Friday. It was for Sheila Roberts. She hadn't been on the council for long, but she had put in more than her fair share of work—more than anyone else on the council, really. She'd gotten elected in her sixties after a long and dedicated career in the local schools.

She was a good woman—probably the member of the Bellwether city council I agreed with the most. I wished she had run for office sooner, honestly. She would have made a good mayor. I wouldn't have hesitated to work for her in any way she'd have me.

Her retirement party wasn't meant to be a huge event. If Sheila had been on the council for longer, it might have been. But as it were, she wasn't at that status in government. There just was no way for her to be, as much as I loved her and her work.

This was more of a formality—a customary, ceremonial event. Pomp and circumstance for the sake of pomp and circumstance. Being that I liked her more than maybe anyone else, I may have been the only one who had to be there who was truly looking forward to it. Aside from her friends and family, everyone else seemed to be going only because they were required to—or at least felt like they were required to. Like swallows to Capistrano, they went because they went.

The day of the banquet I finished work as early as I could. With Mayor Wright's blessing, everyone went home early to get dressed up for the event. There was no practicality in wearing a black gown to work. I would have felt ridiculous—especially considering I tended to feel ridiculous in a gown even in appropriate settings. I suspect Mayor Wright would have felt ridiculous wearing his black tux to a normal workday, too.

I didn't dress up often. That might be obvious at this point. But I didn't. I did, however, own *some* nice clothes. I didn't love stepping out of blue jeans and into a black, floor-length dress and high heels—but sometimes it had to be done. That's life. Sometimes you've got to do things you don't enjoy because sometimes it's just the right thing to do.

I felt better about it because I liked Sheila. And I felt better about it because I wanted to show Theodore that I had that club in my bag, so to speak.

I unashamedly felt good about myself when I dressed up. That's a piece of the point, I guess. Looking nice makes you feel nice. Everyone likes to feel like they look nice—but it sure was physically uncomfortable.

Theodore wasn't ready when I showed up at his place. I was surprised. I expected him, as he almost always was, to be waiting for me, not the other way around. He wasn't, though. In fact, when I rolled up there was no sign of him, so I went up and knocked on his door. It was cracked and I could hear faint sounds coming from within—I couldn't place it, though.

"If that's Jesse, come on in," he hollered back when I knocked. "If you ain't Jesse then get lost."

I smiled—then frowned, thinking about what the hell might happen to anyone who walked into his place and wasn't me. Probably wouldn't be pretty. Theodore wasn't built, but he was tall and fairly toned—leverage, right? Plus, I was willing to bet he had more than one weapon hidden around his place.

"Unabomber, you about ready?" I shouted back when I walked in. I looked around trying to figure out where he was. It was dim in his living room. I paced around, trying to listen for signs that he might be almost ready—a running sink, a zipper being pulled, a closet door closing—but nothing. He didn't respond, either.

I started down the hall toward his bedroom after a long beat. It was getting a little late, and there's no such thing as "fashionably late" at a work event. I took one step toward the bedroom, and he busted out of the door of the hallway bathroom. I thought he was going to knock the door down. He had on that big grin . . . and no tie.

He did have a tie in his hand. I looked at it and made a face.

"Good tie demands a good knot," he said, waving it at me—a colorful plaid number, crisp without wrinkles. "And I haven't gotten it yet, but I work my best under pressure. I'll get it in the car." He winked.

I tried not to let his furious work—the flailing of arms and fabric—be a distraction as I drove, but it absolutely was. I had never worn a tie. I don't know if I'd ever even seen my father in a tie. I must have, but I never saw him tie it. I didn't think it was such a remarkable—or physical—endeavor, but Theodore made it look like he was rewiring a house. He seemed more jittery, more bouncy than usual. I chalked it up to nerves.

The banquet was being held in the high school gym. It was almost distressing how many times I had been there since I graduated so many years before. A symptom of working for the mayor in a small town, I suppose— there just aren't many places to have big events. It's not like our little city hall had a big banquet hall or anything. It barely had enough room for the city council plus a couple of conference rooms for the more important meetings.

Whoever had been in charge of decorating the gym tried their best, but honestly, it still just looked like a gymnasium. They didn't put anything down on the floor, and the tablecloths on the round folding tables were nice, but not *that* nice. The place settings were fine, sure, but they were the same ones we used for every event. Retirement, funeral, award ceremony, inauguration, it didn't matter—same place settings.

As promised, Theodore had gotten his tie done by the time we got there. It was not, to my eye, a particularly remarkable knot. It was symmetrical, I'll grant him that. But otherwise, it was just a fairly nice-looking knot, nothing to write home about.

He was proud, though. Very proud. I was happy he had made himself proud. He told me the tie itself had been his grandfather's. When he gave it to him—after he had retired and claimed to no longer need it—he told him never to wear it without a proper knot. Theodore was determined to keep that promise. So he always took care to get it right, even if it took quite some time.

Ultimately, he gave his grandfather his word, and back there and back then that meant something.

It was a quirk I didn't really expect out of ole Theodore. He always dressed *well*, but I'd never seen him dress *up*. Nor even talk about it, for that matter. As far as I was aware, he was a vaguely grungy, definitely country, quite charming bartender.

I liked it, though. I liked that Theodore had multitudes I couldn't imagine without him revealing them to me. I suppose we all do. I suppose that's the point of being human. But looking back, I can't earnestly claim that Jeff ever surprised me. I knew what I was getting out of him every day and at every phase of our lives. And it was fine. I didn't care at the time and if anything, I liked the predictability of that life after the tumult of my childhood. But I could never lie and say it was great. Not in the way marriage should be.

I think after all I had gone through with Jeff, by the time Theodore and I stepped out of my car dressed to the nines, I was finally ready for some unpredictability. And Theodore was happy to provide it.

He held my hand as we walked into the gym together. I had gotten used to that. I liked his hands. He had a map of the world—or at least Bellwether—on his hands and the tenderness of a man who wants only to give that world all of himself.

* * *

I was alive when my father retired from the military. He claimed it was his decision. He said he was ready to move on and that the military didn't want him to go yet.

He had served since he was eighteen, and he was well north of forty, too old for a soldier. It made sense, in some way, for him to move on to find something else. But for someone so fervently enamored with the military, who loved the war in Vietnam and would have killed more of "the yellow men" if he'd had the chance, I had my suspicions. Then again, I was only seven at the time, what did I know?

Well, what I knew was this: if my father was supposed to be this honorable war hero, why was he getting drunk at his own retirement party?

To figure that out, I guess it makes sense to start earlier. It was in the summer before I turned eight. I spent as much time as our adult guardians would allow with Katie. Life was, as it were, simpler back then—even if my father was as he always was. I took the whoopings and ignored the yelling and showed Katie my bruises with something akin to pride later on.

I don't remember much of the lead up, but I remember him sitting Mom and me down one night and way-too-ceremoniously announcing he was retiring from the military, and there was to be a capital-*C* Celebration in his honor.

I think, looking back, that Mom was immediately skeptical. The only thing she said at first was a slightly drawn out "okaaay."

It was the kind of *okay* that seemed to imply a question mark that she probably didn't want my father to read into. The kind of *okay* that tells its listener, *That's great, but I suspect underlying bullshit.* I cannot confirm whether or not she was actually implying that or whether her *okay* was just a genuine acknowledgment of the announcement. But my memory does tell me that Mom was seldom wrong; she simply wasn't allowed by my father to be right.

They—I'm not sure who *they* were, to be completely honest,—held the "celebration" on a Sunday at one o'clock. I feel like that says something. It was a buffet style luncheon. It wasn't plated steaks and fish and wine and cocktails. It was barbecue from chafing dishes and lemonade from powder. In my seven-year-old mind it was incredible. For the military brass, it was a preposterous affair.

Fitting of my father, they did have beer. Your typical American offerings: cheap, easy to drink, containing alcohol. Shit that gets you intoxicated without feeling like you're drinking. Right up my father's alley. Definitely not classy.

I think that, to be generous, no one else at the ceremony had more than two drinks. It was a Sunday at one. It was barely legal to drink at that time. It certainly wasn't *en vogue* to get hammered.

I remember the collection of empties at my father's table. It was embarrassing, even then. I didn't fully understand. I didn't need to. There's something unspoken and apparent in that visual.

Some folks in uniform spoke in his honor. People I had seen but didn't know. Commanding officers, folks he served with, folks who knew him better than I did. I guess you'd call some of them friends. They said nice enough things. They called my father dedicated and trustworthy. They said he was a pleasure to serve with. They knew he had their back in battle and could lead them out safely. They said . . .

A pleasure to serve with. My father. A pleasure.

He spoke last. That son of a bitch. He was wasted. I wish I didn't remember it. I sure doubt he did.

"Thank you all for coming out to celebrate me" was his opening line. I don't know if the rest of what he said even matters. There isn't really any recovering from that.

Thirteen

One of the more generous parts of a retirement ceremony in the Bellwether High School gym is the honoree gets to choose the decoration theme. Theme, I say loosely. They really just get to pick the color of the cocktail napkins, streamers, and balloons. It's not the most exciting choice. It's not as if they're curating the event—or even choosing its aesthetic, just the colors. But it was something, and in that it was nice.

Sheila picked a lovely shade of light blue. It fit her. She was a steadfast progressive but not in an in-your-face kind of way. She was subtler than that. Kinder. Craftier.

As nice as the event may sound on the surface, it was what it was. There were round tables with cheap tablecloths and no assigned seats. Theodore and I found a table near the middle of the gym—close to the center circle where I did not see many high school basketball games tip off.

Sheila was at the one rectangular table to one side of the gym. She was sitting with her family—it looked like her entire extended family for all of history had come out.

Not even Mayor Wright had been able to score a seat at the head table. It was an impressive display of familial love.

Mayor Wright gave a short toast once it seemed that everyone had grabbed a soda, socialized a bit, and found their way to their seats. He didn't talk for all that long, but he was nice, saying the sort of things you would hope he would say—but not a whole lot more.

Then he invited Sheila to stand and say a few words. A few words it was.

"Thank you, everyone, for being here." She held her hand to her heart. "It is truly humbling to see so many folks I love out here tonight. I have loved my time serving Bellwether, and you all have been like my chosen family."

Sheila then gestured to her loved ones at her table and continued, "Now, I am so grateful to get to spend as much time as I've got left with my blood kin."

Her voice broke as she finished and sat down. The air in the room had turned hot with grand emotion—whether you were close with Sheila or not.

I'm sure there were tears shed. Deservingly so. She hugged her husband beside her, and her youngest grandchild ran up and damn near tackled her from behind before the rest of the kiddos circled around her in a group hug of adoration. I was, for a moment, I hate to admit, a little jealous. I'd never known, and would never know, a family like that.

But then, as sweet as the moment had been, the signal was given that it was time for dinner, the buffet was opened, and the room turned lively again. Smiles went back on faces and tears turned to crinkles at the corners of folks' eyes.

I know it seems like I had frowned upon the buffet at my father's retirement, but that was then. That felt strained. This felt familial. There's a difference.

As folks started to finish their meals, they made their way to have an audience with Sheila. I'm sure it was exhausting for her, but she would have never admitted it. I, too, was one of those people who wanted to talk to her. I joined the queue and watched her treat every person who came up to her like an old friend.

Theodore, despite being a Bellwether native, had never met Sheila. Oh, but he had to—two people like that have got to meet. I made him tag along with me to go talk to her. He was a good sport to play along. I felt a little like I was dragging him around like a dog on a leash or a kid going to meet their kindergarten teacher.

Maybe his feelings didn't max my angst, but my nerves were high. I felt like everyone in the room was looking at me, wondering who this guy was. I had been married, and it hadn't been long—and it's not like I was terribly open about my social life to begin with. I didn't make a big announcement when Jeff left, I just sort of stopped wearing a ring and was honest when people asked. I knew those sorts of rumors spread without their truth's bearer doing any of the leg work.

On top of that, it was a fervent desire of mine to have Sheila like him.

"Jesse!" she exclaimed when we got to the front of the line. "I'm so happy to see you!" She turned to Theodore, then gave me a look, placing her hand knowingly on my arm. "And who is this?"

"Miss Roberts." Theodore extended his hand and gave her that grin. "Theodore Townes. It's an honor to meet you."

"It's good to meet you, Theodore," She accepted his handshake. "But, please, call me Sheila."

"Okay, Miss Roberts." He winked at her. I smiled involuntarily, killing some nerves. You never know when someone is going to make a scene in a bad way—and you sure never want it to be someone you brought. Theodore didn't seem to be doing that, though. Quite the opposite, actually. I liked that.

They chatted for a moment. Theodore answered some questions about what he did and how we met and how come he and Sheila had never met. He was honest, I liked that, too. But it did make me nervous. I wasn't sure if she would frown on me seeing someone like him.

Not that there was something wrong with someone like him. I hate the way "someone like him" sounds altogether. But still, she was on the city council, and he worked at a bar. I think my worry was natural. Maybe not.

After the idle chitchat had been exhausted and Theodore had held court for long enough with Sheila, I leaned in to give her a hug and congratulate her on her retirement. She leaned into my right ear, to the opposite side of Theodore.

"Keep him around, Jesse," she said. "He's a good one, honey. Keep him around." She gave me a big smile and a kiss on the cheek.

If I needed approval of dating Theodore, there it was. There weren't many opinions in Bellwether I respected as much. Fewer who were alive. Bill, and maybe Mayor Wright, were on the list. As it so happens, they were both in the room, too.

Fourteen

As logical as it had been to move in with Katie after Mom died, it wasn't easy. I wanted my Mom to be alive—I wished it had been my father who'd died. There was nothing I could do to erase what had just happened or to extract myself from my reality and place myself into the one I wished to live in. The future I wanted to dream of was gone—it was never going to happen.

I was a junior in high school. I should've been excited. I should've been looking forward to graduating next year, to the future. I wasn't. There simply was no future in my mind. I couldn't imagine one anymore. In a way, that's a good thing—I couldn't misimagine one, but part of me needed a future to dream up, no matter how unattainable it might have been.

The first night at Katie's was particularly hard. I had never slept in a bed other than the one in my parents' house while knowing I wouldn't be returning home. That's not an easy concept to grapple with. I had slept over with Katie but with the quiet comfort of knowing that the momentary discomfort of sleeping in an unfamiliar place was maybe only a moment.

As terrible as life in a house with my father had been, I knew what I was getting. I could get to sleep there. Back then, I would recognize my surroundings when I woke up at three in the morning because I'd had a nightmare that I killed my father. *Nightmare*—what a word.

I didn't recognize my surroundings on a mattress on the floor in Katie's bedroom. The sheets weren't mine; the mattress's indents weren't my form. Sleeping at her house that first night, I knew it wasn't only a moment. For the foreseeable future, it was my life.

I remember dreaming a recursive visual lament of awaking in my childhood bed, again and again—waking to find the reality I had was no longer. I dreamed I had a good and happy family. I dreamed and I dreamed; and I awoke and I awoke. And every time I did, I was on a mattress on my best friend's floor, and it was better than getting yelled at by my father, but I couldn't help but feel ashamed in myself that I felt jealous of Mom.

Things got better that first morning. I moved on a weekend—an effort for an easier transition. It was a good thought. It was a sunny day so the light peeking through the shades woke us up in the early hours of day.

The air smelled sweet. It was familiar, but different. Coffee, but not my father's. I wasn't a coffee drinker then, but Katie's mom made a pot every morning. I learned to have a full mug with breakfast. It felt like the nice thing to do. I learned to only associate the smell of coffee with her. Still do. Funny how memories work.

Katie's mom had made coffee and scrambled eggs and waffles in her antique-looking waffle iron. It wasn't necessarily the most delicious breakfast I'd ever had, but at that point, I think I appreciated it more than any one previous. She had made the effort to make food for us. My father had never done that. Mom had tried, but never this well, and never without my father yelling about something he thought she'd gotten wrong.

"Do you all want to go to the art museum today?" Katie's mom asked when we sat down at the table. Her dad was off in Richmond for the weekend for business.

We were obviously getting older—getting, in a way, smarter—but we were hardly intellectuals. I had never been to an *art* museum—hell, I couldn't be sure I had ever been to any kind of museum at all. Maybe on a field trip in elementary school, but I didn't remember it.

"The one in Roanoke has a new exhibit showing some van Goghs. I read about it in the paper," she continued. "It looked interesting. It might be the kind of thing you can tell your teachers about to earn some brownie points, too. But that's not a reason to go!" She punctuated the line with a finger raised in near mimicry of herself. "A reason to go is that it's enriching."

She looked back down at the waffle she was working on, as if she wasn't sure she believed herself—but she sure was trying to. I wasn't particularly interested in going to look at art. Art seemed pretentious to me—and it still does a lot of the time. But say what you will for the specifics, I appreciated the effort. I was willing to humor it. Katie's eyeroll told me she was less willing to humor it.

We went, anyway, leaving shortly after breakfast—careful to take enough time to get dressed, although not enough time for Katie to talk her mom out of it.

The exhibit was interesting enough. The paintings were good, I guess. I didn't, I don't, and I will never know much about art—but these were famous paintings, and I could tell why. There was something unspoken about them that we all liked.

I wasn't drawn to the paintings, though. I was drawn to a plaque with a biography of Vincent van Gogh—his history of mental illness and institutionalization, the birth of *The Starry Night* from a hard time of life but yet becoming his master work and a known symbol around the world. Particularly, I was drawn to the question of his death: did he kill himself or was he murdered?

It made me think of Mom. The despair she must have felt. I wondered if there had been a dream in her, waiting to be awoken. I would never get to know. Maybe she'd never had one. Maybe it makes more sense that way. Vincent van Gogh is still famous, so he must have had something the rest of us just don't.

I thought of my father, too. He was so troubled. I didn't want him to be evil, or maybe I did. Either way, I think he might have been. *Evil*—what a hideous word. Did he have something to show the world that he couldn't? He did, after all, grow up in the Bellwether where everyone went to the military whether you liked it or not, and the other option was being shunned. He went to war and was evil while he was there. He was evil, as I learned painfully, when he got back. But what is evil, anyway? Evil might be subjective, I don't know.

I wondered if I had something to show the world. If there was art in me waiting to explode. If a seed might be planted by Mom's dying that may someday bloom. Probably not, I figured.

You can't really explain, you can't really know, you can't really feel a van Gogh until you see it in real life. When you see those brush strokes up close you can feel what he had felt. I wondered if he really killed himself or if that boy did. I hoped that boy did, to be honest. In that reality, he's kind of the hero. That boy wasn't good to him, but van Gogh protected them. That's nice, in a way. If he died by self-inflicted gunshot, it's just a tragedy. *Just* a tragedy.

* * *

"Where'd you learn to schmooze like that?" I asked Theodore as we left the gym after Sheila's retirement celebration. A duet of owls caterwauling echoed off the hills into the night.

"I'd say it's just how my mama raised me. But honestly"—he smirked at me—"working at the bar. You learn how to talk to anyone and how to seem like you don't dislike anyone, even when it ain't true. So I guess when you get to talk to people you really like, it's even easier."

I chuckled and blushed.

"So what's the worst experience you've ever had in the bar?" I asked, then added. "Please, God, don't say meeting me."

"Oh no, meeting you is number one for sure." He looked at me with that damn grin. "Umm . . ." He looked up into the star-speckled sky, thinking. "There have been some doozies, but the worst has to be a, let me say, very intentionally unnamed head football coach who came through on a recruiting visit.

"The guy was a jackass in the goddamn truest sense. Came here to scout a kid at the high school he ain't even offer a walk-on spot to in the end. Ridiculous."

I let the quiet be my tacit beg for the story to continue.

"Anyway, it's late, like, maybe one-thirty. Coach gets into town late, decides to grab a beer. Whatever, not that unusual. Folks come in late all the time, and we do get folks in here on business sometimes.

"Problem was, this motherfucker walks in like everyone in the room is going to stop and look in awe of him. He's got his team polo on, cocksure grin, the works. He kind of struts in and looks around like *All right, which of you poor fucks is gonna ask for my autograph first?* Now, mind you, it's me and a bunch of the regulars in there. It's a Thursday, high school ballgame on a Friday—not too many of us were too inclined to go to the games, anyway.

"Not only does no one in the room care that he's there. No one has a goddamn clue who he was. He strolls over, orders a double neat of this vintage bourbon. Not the nicest tasting, but expensive as all get out. I get it for him; he complains that the double ain't a double. Whatever, I splash a little more. Fine.

"The guy sits there drinking for maybe an hour. Whole time he's looking around, just waiting—no no, he is *hoping* someone will recognize him and, I dunno, beg him for attention like a dog looking for a treat? Of course, no one does. It's not like he was from a Virginia school, either. Not a local. Big national name but unless you're a real football fan, you wouldn't know, either.

"Finally, he's done, and I bring him his check. He starts whining, wants it free, wants a discount, wants this, that, and the other 'cause I was rude, and I didn't pour a full double, and the atmosphere sucked, and the patrons were rude. Whatever. Any excuse he could come up with.

I told him, 'Tough shit, fella. You aren't in the big city anymore.'

"Eventually, he agrees to pay. Tips like shit. I think it was something like 4 percent on a hundred-dollar check. Absolutely nuts.

"Well, I'm taking his payment and see the name on the card, and that's when I realized who it was." He paused finally and looked at me, smiling. "So, yeah, that fucker was the worst."

"Well, I guess I can see how I might have been better than that." I gave him a kiss.

* * *

Things were fine for a while after I moved in with Katie. We were still best friends and talked all the time. We went everywhere together—even more so once we started living together. But then suddenly, we didn't.

It started one evening when, upon returning home from school, Katie told me she had plans with some other folks. She didn't say I wasn't invited, but I could read between the lines. She didn't even tell me who she was going out with. I knew, of course, that she had friends aside from me. I had friends aside from her—a few of them, anyway. But it was a rare day that I ever did anything with them without Katie being there, too.

Katie's dad was out for work, but Katie's mom was home and cooked supper for us. Just the two of us. Two strangers passing by each other in a strange moment of circumstance. Not mother and daughter but, in a way, the closest thing to it that either of us had at the moment.

It was no secret to me that Katie and her mom weren't real close. Not that that is uncommon for high school kids. But I had reached a point in my life where it saddened me a bit. I didn't have a mom to fight with. I just had a father I hated and would never see again—willingly. I missed Mom more than I had missed anything in my life. To be honest, I didn't know until then that I had that emotion.

Katie's mom and I sat in uncomfortable quiet that night. Rarely looking up from our plates, we tried our best to cover the pain. Her pain sure was real, too. Her daughter was alive, but a parent can't help but miss their baby when they grow up and drift off.

Katie finally came home late that night. She seemed off, but I couldn't place it. She didn't have bloodshot eyes, she wasn't stumbling in drunk, but she was definitely off. I had known her long enough to see that.

"What's up K?" I asked her, trying to sound as light as I could. "Have a good time?"

"Not too bad," she said blankly. "Not too bad."

Her mom rolled her eyes and left the room. She had been standing in the doorway when Katie came home and now walked to her bedroom. I didn't know what she knew. I didn't know if she knew anything. Looking back, she knew enough.

"What were you doing?" I half whispered and it came out a little harsh.

"Nothing. We just hung out and watched some TV."

"Katie"—I leaned into her face trying to get a real answer—"we hang out here and watch TV all the damn time. Hell, we hang out with our friends and watch TV all the time. This ain't that."

"We were really just watching TV and chilling," she said, sternly this time. I noticed that she wouldn't look me in the eye. I had never known Katie to avoid looking me in the eye.

All the same, I decided it would be best to drop it for the night. She clearly wasn't going to tell me anything, and I frankly didn't know for certain if there was anything to know, and I didn't want to push her and be wrong.

Besides, the fight wasn't worth it. Her mom seemed upset, and I knew from experience it wasn't good to be in a house where neither person with you will talk to you. We went into our room and watched TV without talking. We still needed each other, I guess. Me as much as her, and her as much as me.

The next Friday at school, I passed a note to Katie as I had done so many times before: *bike to house today?*

I expected a nod. She never said no to going out and exploring. Instead, she wrote down a note and passed it back. I thought it might be a joke or something else—an excited affirmation of our plans.

Instead: *can't – plans*

I stared at the note for a moment then balled it up and stuffed it into my jacket pocket. She didn't make eye contact with me for the rest of that period—like a dog who got into something she shouldn't have, she knew she had done something I wouldn't like. But it wasn't that, exactly. It wasn't anger. It was that first biting breeze in November that tells you winter is coming, that the comfort of fall and the quaint peace it brings are making way for something cold and dark. December, when it comes, is spiteful; and December was coming.

I tried to act like everything was normal the rest of the day. Katie and I went to the rest of our classes and chatted casually. Small talk was easy at school—mostly complaining about this class or that, this assignment or that. After school Katie and I walked up together, and for a minute, I thought she just might go with me. She didn't.

"See you at home?" she asked as we got on our bikes. She sounded normal, probably felt normal. I did not. And *home* was an interesting word. It was hers to keep; I never really knew mine.

"Okay," I said. I had found over the years that the word *okay* works to fill most situations in which you don't know what to say. It was the word for the liminal space between conversation and avoidance. That moment was one of them. I fiddled with my helmet for a while, pretending to adjust the straps as if they hadn't always stayed the same, and watched as Katie rode away from me to meet her friends.

Well, if she won't go hang out at the house with me anymore, I'll go myself. It would be quiet out there, at least. A place for my own thoughts.

"Fuck it," I huffed to myself as I slammed down on my bike pedal and took off toward the woods.

I hammered my legs as fast as they would go the whole way there. It was an unusually warm day, and the wind whipping over my face felt good. I liked the pain in my quads. Not pain, exactly, but discomfort. A discomfort I could control. A discomfort not within my soul, but within my terrestrial form. A discomfort I could take solace in knowing would go away moments after I stopped it.

As fast as I could muster, I rode, flying down sidewalks, then eventually the bike path. I took the long way—the way that had lower grade hills, fewer turns, more straightaways. Put another way, I took the route that allowed me to go as recklessly fast as I wanted. I didn't notice people around me as I pedaled.

They were there, but I didn't care. I didn't care that they wanted me to slow down. I didn't care that they jumped when they heard me coming past—a little too late.

I would've hit them if I wasn't in such control. I didn't care about the few who flipped me the bird or spit a curse my way. I fucking pedaled, and I wasn't in Bellwether, I wasn't anywhere, I wasn't me.

I slowed down as I turned toward the fire road, and I didn't notice the freshly beaten-down weeds and shrubbery. We hadn't been to the house since I moved in with Katie. I was just excited to go back.

I didn't notice the new graffiti on the trestle as I walked over. Graffiti that tainted the once unvarnished, if old, structure. I didn't notice the path was worn in a way that swore the truth that people had come and gone plenty since I had last. I didn't notice I was sweating through the jacket I had worn to school but certainly no longer needed.

I pulled up to the house balancing with one foot on one pedal. I let my bike drift to the right of the path and felt the pull of the grass in the spokes. I looked off into the woods and hopped off the bike, coming to a trot, then a walk, then a stop.

I heard voices. I was sure I heard voices. I walked a little bit closer and turned my gaze to the front door of the house. As I neared it was clear—there were people inside the house. People who were not me. People who were not invited by me. Others—at our place.

That's when I noticed the bikes leaning on the side of the house. I had missed them as I cruised up. I didn't miss them now. I thought I might recognize one of them. I couldn't be sure.

The voices hadn't died down or changed cadence, so I knew they hadn't heard me. Still, I didn't dare to inch any closer. I needed to not be heard—so I hid myself from auditory view and walked backward with my bike. I was suddenly aware of the sweat inching down my cheeks and dampening my jacket, making it stick to my back. Aware of the tamped down plants, clearly defining several rows of bikes gone by. Aware of the new graffiti on the side of the house, though I couldn't quite make it out.

Nerves had my legs and arms shaking, and I worried that if I tried to turn around and hop on the bike I might fall.

If I fell, I might make noise. More noise meant more odds of being discovered by whomever was in the house. I didn't want that. I didn't know who was there. I didn't know if they might be dangerous. I didn't want to be a story, a horror story—a body in the woods—a story of a house and a crime destined to remain something of a mystery, legend. A legend told down the mountain years past my expiration—one in which I'm given a name not mine and made to be a hapless foal traipsed into the lair of the beast. I was not going to let that story merge with mine, so I moved slowly, carefully.

I walked maybe halfway back to the trestle before I got back on my bike. I hauled ass back down. I didn't stop at the trestle and walk my bike over—I was willing to risk the fall. Maybe by that point I wanted to fall.

I could be sure my legs would get cut up by the blackberry bushes and various other underbrush, but I didn't care. I was heaving, searching for air by the time I made it to the greenway. I didn't let myself catch my breath fully before I started down the greenway again toward Katie's house. Her home, not mine. There weren't many red lights between where I was and where I was going, but I didn't stop for them, anyway.

When I got there, I felt tired. The burn in my quads and the hurt in my lungs started to set in as I walked up to the front door. I had my breath back, more or less. I didn't want to seem too frazzled in front of Katie's mom when I came in.

Fortunately, she was out back, piddling around with the beginnings of turning their garden around for the coming spring. I snuck in without her seeing me and went straight to the bathroom.

I hadn't looked down since the woods, and when I finally got to the bathroom and plopped down on the toilet, the damage from my sprint was obvious. There were streams of drying blood down my lower legs. I couldn't see where the cuts were—though I wasn't sure if that was because they were small, or there were so many of them. Either way, the blood was obvious, and it was a lot to clean.

In lieu of using an entire roll of toilet paper to painstakingly clean myself up, I settled for a shower. Good thing, too. I probably looked horrendous. Sweaty, hair out of whack and sticking to my face. I looked like I'd been through an ordeal, so I let the water soak me and slowly wash away the signs.

The blood, though, as it were, had started to dry. It looked as though my legs had begun to rust, and onto that was caked a layer of deep red. It took more scrubbing—and a whole lot more stinging than I wanted—to get it all off my skin. I washed the wounds, there were plenty, with a bar of soap, hoping to avoid infection. I didn't know a lot about infectious disease, but I had heard about staph infections, and they didn't sound fun.

I patted my legs dry carefully to avoid more pain, but I felt it, anyway. I opened the cabinet to grab some bandages, but it was soon apparent it would take an entire box to cover all of the open wounds on my legs. Not prudent, I figured.

I wrapped myself in a towel and slinked on light toes to the room Katie and I shared. I grabbed a pair of black yoga pants in an effort to hide any more blood that might seep from the many open slits.

Glad it wasn't summer, I finally walked out to the living room and sat on the couch. Katie's mom had come inside and greeted me when she saw me.

"Hey, Jesse. How was school?"

"It was okay. The usual stuff." I didn't look up.

"That's good." I could hear her smile. "Is Katie with you?"

"No." I hesitated, trying to read the moment. "She said she had plans after school."

"Ah." I heard her smile fade. She sighed. "Okay."

She didn't say any more and eventually worked her way back outside. The garden was a good place to escape, I suppose. I would have joined her out there if I knew her any better. Not that I didn't know her well, but things were, obviously, different than they had been when I was little. We hadn't had that kind of talk since Mom died. She had known my parents and me for as long as Katie and I had been friends, for those long and formative years, and until that day, I hadn't considered that there may have been some grief for her, too, in Mom's passing.

Katie and I didn't talk much that night. I had a hand I didn't want to play. She probably thought she had a full house and that I hadn't even been dealt in. We were both wrong.

I knew one thing for sure, though—the bike at the house that day had been hers.

Fifteen

I really only have one good memory of my father. I was real little, maybe six, maybe younger. I can't remember the exact timeline of my early life, so bear with me, please. Either way, as I recall it, I was real little. Little enough that I didn't have significant thoughts of my own, little enough that I didn't hate my father yet.

It was a particularly cold fall, back when it was harder to get folks to believe in the climate reality. Cool air has that effect on you; cool air makes things seem okay. It made things seem okay that day. That's how I remember it.

My father decided that fall that he wanted to get back into hunting. He had, according to the tales he told, hunted with his father as a kid. He wanted, he told me, to pass those memories on to me. I was young enough that I wanted him to, too.

I don't even know if my father had a hunting license. I certainly didn't—then again, I was young enough that I didn't know that I needed one. I know he didn't practice firing his gun before we went. It was an old gun, a well-worn 12-gauge his father had given him when he was old enough. It had been in the house my whole life. Never locked up, it just lived in its case in the closet in my folks' room. Trigger locks were not a thought in our household.

There was a sizable plot of public game lands near Bellwether where most folks who hunted—which was most folks in town, really—went during the fall. To get a good spot you had to get there early, and you had to hike deep into the woods. Competition was fierce.

Most folks who were too lazy to get there on time were also the kind of folks who were too lazy to walk too far into the woods. It worked out because hunting etiquette demands that, when arriving late, you absolutely do not trudge past someone else's hunting spot because one, you probably smell because you didn't get up in time to shower with scent-free soap, wash your clothes, or mask the scents on your boots—my father and I used pine needles—and two, stomping through, no matter how light you think you're stepping, is loud enough to scare off any deer that could be in the area.

No one walks softly enough to muffle the sound of a dried maple leaf shattering under foot. Not even the coyotes, not even the squirrels.

My father told me he had gone scouting during the week while I was at school and had found a good spot for us to go, but we had to get there real early. If we didn't get there in time we'd miss out, and if we missed out, the chances of seeing a deer became much lower. I had no reason not to believe him. This was the kind of thing he was actually inclined to be truthful about—and he was.

The spot he found was on the northeast side of the plot and backed up to a neighboring trailer park, Whistling Heights, with just enough buffer for the folks who lived there not to disrupt us. He said we would make a ground blind right at the edge of the game lands with our backs to the Heights so no deer could sneak up on us.

We would see anything coming, and the deer would be used to any noise we might make, being so close to the Heights where folks made a lot of noise at all hours. "Good shooting lanes, too," he said.

I was up before my father that morning. Instincts, I guess. Maybe a false memory but I swear I remember being awake when I heard his alarm going off. I have half a mind to think I was already getting dressed when he got up, though I doubt that's true.

It was still dark out, more night than morning. He had laid out a set of camouflage pants, socks, a shirt, and a sweatshirt for me. He told me not to put on the sweatshirt until we go into the woods, so I wouldn't sweat too much.

All of the clothes were meant for boys, from a time before I was born when my father was hoping I'd come out with a penis—despite seeing the ultrasound saying otherwise. I didn't care, anyhow. I was young and determined, and they ought to have been unisex, anyway. I wanted to please my father still, and maybe that pleased him all the same.

He gave me a green bottle of scent-free body wash to use. It said scent-free, anyway. As I showered with it, I thought it smelled awful. But it's label, adorned with promises of fruitful hunts—images of antlers and scopes and a vague camo pattern—sold me on its use.

He gave me a scent-free deodorant stick to use, the first time in my life I used deodorant. It did, however, truly smell of nothing. I rolled on the white salve and felt the invisibility it was to provide. I rubbed my arms against my sides, something like a cricket, feeling the deodorant rub in and dry.

Piece-by-piece I put on the camo, and all of it felt stiff, from shirt to pants, stodgy and never worn. I felt clunky and misshapen. It must've been how David Byrne felt in that suit.

I rolled the wool socks he'd given me up my legs and liked the soft feeling they gave me—I didn't like them as much once I put my boots on and started walking. Wool socks aren't as comfortable when they're sweaty.

My father's truck hurled cold air at me when he started it up. He had a hot coffee for himself and a thermos of hot cocoa for me—a special, rare-occasion kind of treat of my youth. My father didn't seem to mind the cold, if anything, he embraced it.

I wrapped the sweatshirt around my knees as a blanket to stop their shaking. That helped, as much as it could. In my memory it must have been something less than ten degrees outside that morning. Realistically, it was probably in the midthirties.

It was still dark when my father pulled the truck into a gravel lot I didn't recognize. There was one other truck already there, but he told me it was broken down and had been there for weeks. It looked like it, too, with its flat front tires and leaves accumulated over the hood. A film of algal scum had begun to grow on the windshield, a sign of the times. I wondered if anyone was going to come back to get it. Doubtful, I think, looking back. It was probably towed and impounded, scrapped for parts, eventually.

The ground sounded frozen when I stepped out of the truck. The dirt and gravel under my boots crunched, and the fallen leaves were white and crisp with frost. Ice crystals raised the dirt, soon to turn back to mud with the rising run.

I walked around outside the truck trying to find the most satisfying crunch while my father got ready. He slung the gun over one shoulder and a backpack over the other.

"Ready?" he said. I walked up to him and stood ironically at attention. "Remember, walk softly, and if you have to say something, whisper." He lowered his head and raised his shoulders in mock quiet stance with a finger to his lower lip.

I nodded and pursed my lips with might, symbolically showing my silence. I followed him toward an opening in the wood line and fell in line behind him as gravel turned to dirt and fallen leaves. I tried to place my small boots into his giant footprints. Being so young, I didn't do so well. I was a foal in the wake of a stallion. I'm sure I was being loud. I'm sure I crashed hard yet onto every new pile of leaves we came across. My father didn't make me feel bad about it. He knew, for a moment, that I didn't mean to be loud. I was trying my best. Maybe he was, too.

As he promised, it was a long trudge to the spot he had chosen. It seemed like we would never reach a destination, but we did. In the still-dim woods it was hard to get my bearings—the early morning light hadn't yet begun to cut through the trees. My father walked over to a spot between two trees, large pines close together—his landmark—and rested the gun at the base of one.

He used his boots to clear the leaves from a spot between the trees until the dirt beneath was bare and soft, a little damp, but importantly quiet. He whispered for me to sit, so I did. Even through all of my layers, the ground was cold, but I assumed my position obediently, anyway. I hadn't walked all that way to give up now.

In the growing light of the early morning, I watched my father gather a pair of discarded Christmas trees from the edge of the woods. Remnants from holidays past in the Heights. He stacked them, facing opposite directions, leaning against the towering, long leaf pines so that they created a wall in front of us. The Christmas trees had been there for a while and were losing their needles, but they did enough.

After he had them set just so, he found some branches from around the woods and propped them against the front of the wall, for further cover. He didn't mind the space behind us. Nothing would come from back there, from the neighborhood, he said.

Once the wall was set, he came back to me and cleared more leaves, creating a patch of dirt for him to sit on. From his backpack he pulled out two pairs of binoculars—a nice pair and a cheap pair, one for him and one for me—and then a blanket. He handed me the blanket and told me not to freeze. I smiled, shivering, as beams of light started to come through the branches of the trees above.

He sat down and grabbed the shotgun. He pulled a box of buckshot from the backpack and loaded the gun. Then we sat.

* * *

I got to school early on a Tuesday, not long after the incident at the house. Katie had a doctor's appointment—her last annual physical of grade school— so she told me to go on ahead. Of course, it took me less time than usual to get out the door and get to school. I was sitting alone in the class with my first period teacher, Mrs. Rodwell.

She wasn't my favorite teacher, and I didn't know her well, but to her credit she cared about all of her students the same, which is to say, intensely, no matter what.

I was doodling in a notebook, waiting for someone else to join me in the room. Mrs. Rodwell was at her desk grading tests—she was a dedicated teacher and good at what she did, but all of her tests were multiple choice. I hated multiple choice tests. I never did well on them. I hadn't done well on the ones she was grading that day, and she knew it.

Done with the stack she was working on, she stood up and walked to me. She leaned against a table at the front of the class and folded her arms.

"What are you planning to do after graduation, Jesse?" she asked inquisitively. I could tell she was leading the conversation somewhere.

Spring was coming, and I still had no plans for what to do after school was over. Honestly, in my mind, the world didn't exist after I graduated—at least not with me in it yet. I didn't want to think about what life might look like after the one reliable system of support I had left—the one that no one could legally take from me—was no longer.

Katie and I were still hanging out, but it felt strained. Even if I was just imagining it that way, the strain was real to me. She seemed different, but I didn't want to address it. I couldn't lose the one friend I had left and lose the structure of school, all in one fell swoop. This was made a particularly dreadful predicament by the sheer fact that one of those things, by default, would be imminently going away.

"Um, no plans yet."

"That's what I thought," she responded, measured, not trying to sound too eager. "Well, my sister actually runs the Motel 6 up on Oliver Street. You could start before graduation even—if you wanted. Nothing too glamorous. Just front desk work, but it pays okay, and with your intelligence, you'd be pretty good at it—I doubt you'd end up being there long before finding something better."

I didn't respond right away. In part of my mind, I hated the thought of just working at the front desk of the motel, but to the rest of me, it seemed like a stable job and a fair opportunity. I wanted structure, and lo and behold, it presented itself.

"That actually sounds pretty nice," I said. I wasn't lying, exactly, but the idea of being thrust into the real world made my stomach uneasy.

"Good." Mrs. Rodwell smiled warmly. "I'll give you her number so you can get in contact with her."

A couple of my classmates had filed in while we were talking. They didn't seem to care what we were talking about—or maybe they were just being polite.

At any rate, Mrs. Rodwell made good and handed me a slip of paper before she started class with a phone number on it. I folded it and stuck it into my back pocket. I wanted to call right then, but I would have to practice patience—something I would learn I ought to get used to.

Katie rolled into class late and took her seat beside me. "What was that?" she said when Mrs. Rodwell handed me the number.

"Nothing," I lied, dismissively.

Katie took the cue and turned back to her desk. As she leaned down to her backpack to grab out a notebook, her blazing mass of hair covered her face, and for a moment she looked like the wild-haired child I had befriended at an early age. I wanted to go back, then. It had seemed simpler before—*little kids, little problems; big kids, big problems*, they say. Because it's true.

After school Katie asked again, "What was the note Mrs. R handed you?"

"It was a phone number," I said as we unlocked our bikes. "Her sister runs the Motel 6 and might give me a job."

"Oh nice," she said, her face betraying her surprise. "That would be pretty nice . . ." She paused. "If you could land a good job already, that is."

"Yeah."

Sixteen

"Hear that?" my father hissed in a low whisper.

I did hear it. A sharp crunch. Different from the sound squirrels make as they shuffle through the leaves and up and down trees. Softer than the heavy foot of a fellow hunter trekking through the forest. I didn't know the sound well, but I knew it was different.

My father motioned to his eyes, then off into the woods in the distance, pointing to something neither he nor I could see yet. The steps got louder, progressively louder. Then I saw movement in the liminal gaps between the trunks of towering trees, a blur of brown fur. A deer.

It was walking toward us from the left, right into the clear area thirty yards to our front. It's pace was slow but steady, relaxed. The deer was not on alert for danger; it was just moving through the forest as it always did. But it was, unknowingly, walking right into my father's line of fire.

As the deer got closer, I could see it clearly. A buck. A young one. Six pointer, maybe. It wasn't big, but on the public lands you took what you could. There wasn't much to take—the animals tended to be smarter than the hunters out there.

If we were hunting on private lands and we were serious hunters, we would have let him pass and grow into a mature buck worthy of putting on the wall of a log cabin. But we were not in that situation. Far from it. And I don't think most of the folks in those woods had any interest in that more sophisticated, privileged brand of hunting, anyway.

My father readied his gun, getting his grip just right, like a hustler might work a cue stick on the break of a big-money game at a pool hall. The deer kept walking. My father motioned to me to cover my ears, holding his calloused hands cupped to the side of his head, then raised his gun and waited. The deer kept walking, sharply crunching leaves under foot with each tantalizing step. Then it stopped. My father steadied.

I had heard gunshots before, but never that close. Gunfire was a constant up in the mountains—it seemed like some sort of animal was always in season, so the hunt never stopped. From miles away the echo of a shotgun is background noise. Gunfire from a foot away is different. It makes you respect the power of the blast, the danger of the weapon.

The deer turned ninety degrees and high tailed it away from us, a flash of white tail dashing away like a shooting star in the fleeting night. My father put a finger to his lips, telling me to remain quiet, and turned his right ear toward the forest ahead after the white of the deer's tail disappeared into the brush. He was waiting for the crash of a dying deer hitting the ground, but it never came. He looked down, listening intently and thinking to himself, then sighed.

"Okay," he whispered with a heavy exhale. "Let's wait a minute then go after it."

"Why do we have to wait?" My youthful self was impatient and didn't quite understand that most hunts didn't involve only an hour of waiting for a deer. I was ready to go. I didn't get it.

"Don't want to jump it," my father explained, still looking off into the forest. "Want to give it time to bleed out if it's still alive."

The words made sense, but the concept was lost on me. He shot the deer. It should be dead, and we should be able to go get it. Bullets kill; that's how I had understood it. It turns out it doesn't work that way. Who knew? My father, I guess. At least a little bit.

A few excruciating minutes later he said, "Okay." He rose, and I stood up eagerly at attention to his side. There were knots in my stomach from the wait, quietly sitting beside my father, paying attention to nothing. They untied as we walked away from our Christmas tree blind. The hunt, for me, felt on.

I followed my father out toward where the deer had been standing when he shot.

"Look for blood," he whispered, a little louder than he had been, pointing to the ground where there were some rustled up leaves. His volume told me the stalking phase was over. This was no longer about visibility; it was about tracking the deer by any means necessary.

I didn't really know what I was looking for but went through the motions anyway. The forest floor looked like a forest floor. Browns and tans and oranges and, most importantly, reds of soon-to-be winter leaves.

"Here!" He almost sounded excited as he pointed to a tiny dot of bright red blood on a light brown oak leaf. My father never sounded excited in that way, almost gleeful. It was a new tone for me, and I never heard it again after that day. "And here!" He pointed again to another spot of blood a couple of feet away, in the general direction the buck ran. "Okay, this is what we're looking for. Now we just have to follow the trail until we find him." He made it sound so simple.

"Oh, I found one!" I squealed, but my father politely informed me it was just a red spot on a fall leaf. He found a new drop and pointed out what the real thing looks like, how it looks wet and the slight reflection of sunlight. The difference was mostly lost on me.

We tracked the blood for maybe a hundred yards, and the splotches of blood got thicker and more frequent. It seemed like we must be getting close. I vividly remember how my heart rate rose with anticipation, sure that we'd see a heap of dead fur soon.

But we didn't, and the blood led us into a thicker patch of forest. Soon we were ducking under branches, even me with my seven-year-old frame, so imagine how my father had to limbo and step over fallen logs. The trees were younger but closer together and the oak leaves gave way to thicker, more uniform but bearing less flat surface pine needles, which made the blood splotches harder to spot, but still we trudged on. I followed diligently behind as my father, kneeling down as he stalked along, found one red spot after the other.

He seemed not to notice the thickening forest; he was on a mission. I was seven, so I wasn't bothered, either, but I certainly noticed. The terrain was getting hard to pass. Tucked among the pines were briars, and soon I could feel a sting on my legs. My thin children's pants were no match for the hard and brilliant thorns. Those weather-hardened thorns cut clean. Still, I followed along.

I followed along for probably another hour. We went surely miles beyond where we started, but still we found no deer. We spotted a few other hunters in their various perches and courteously skirted along them. Some of them pointed us the way of the bleeding deer that ran by, but we never saw that deer again, and we were never going to. We had to make the walk of misery back to the truck. Empty handed and defeated. I understood that.

"I must not have put a good shot on him." My father sighed as he leaned against the tailgate. I didn't know exactly what that meant. His hair stuck slightly to his forehead from the sweat that broke thick as we walked. He had finally called off the search as the blood was getting thinner and farther apart. I never lost hope, but I could see it drained from him in real time.

In reality, he had gutshot that buck. It would die, surely, but slowly and not in a place where we would ever find it. It would suffer, and it would die. I see that now.

All of this, not for lack of giving my father a good shot—a better marksman would've taken that deer down ten times out of ten. Practice, in hunting, does pay off. Not taking your gun to the range for the better part of a decade and then going out and hoping for the best, not so much.

My father packed his gear back up in the truck, careful to put it all back as he had set it in the morning. I went to sit in the passenger seat and noticed that my pants looked different. They were open in places, holes cut from thorns, and they were stained with blood—not the deer's blood, but mine. Not a lot, but enough that it was plainly visible. I panicked trying to figure out how I might hide it from my father; I assumed he would be mad at me. I didn't want to get a whooping for staining his pants, but I was locked in, and he was coming to the truck. I had to take what I had coming.

He sat down and turned the key, not noticing the blood at first, but then he did.

"Oh my God," he said, genuinely horrified. "Jesse, are you okay?"

"Oh, yeahhh," I said naively. "I think I got cut by the thorns."

"Well here." He handed me his jacket. "Put pressure on the cuts. Let's get you home and get you cleaned up. You don't want those getting infected."

My father sat me on the toilet when we got home and helped me tug off my boots. Hunting boots don't like coming off with sweaty wool socks, but with a pull and a twist my legs were free. I took off my pants and felt nauseated when I saw dried blood mixed with sweat, highlighted by weaving lines of crimson scratches from my thighs to my ankles.

My father stayed calm, though, and used a wad of wet toilet paper to wipe my legs clean. Then he took another wad of toilet paper and doused it with a little rubbing alcohol. Goodness, it stung, I damn sure remember that, but my father told me it would keep me from getting infection.

He told me there were too many cuts to try to cover them all, no use in using that many bandages.

"We'll just put a thin layer of Neosporin over your whole legs," he told me as he put a dab on his finger and showed me how to gently apply it to my wounds. "Just don't use too much, or it'll get all over everything when it gets warm—and that sure is a pain to clean, I tell you what." He smiled. He had a charming smile; he just didn't use it often.

He handed me the tube of ointment and let me lather my legs the rest of the way. It felt slimy and gross, but it soothed the sting.

I swung my little legs sitting on the toilet to get them to dry while my father went to get me a clean pair of shorts to put on. I could hear Mom in the kitchen cooking—she hadn't greeted us when we came in. She didn't know my father was in a good mood. He wasn't in one often.

He helped me clean up the mess we'd made and gave me the tube of Neosporin to reapply before bed. He gave me a kiss on the forehead and tousled my hair. He certainly didn't do everything right that morning, but I never did get an infection.

I think I also understood my father a little more, looking back from that day. He couldn't get out of his own damn way, that was true, but he hadn't been dealt the prettiest hand, either. I think that maybe, if I can give him that kind of generosity, he never did get over his own struggles. Even when Mom was alive, he couldn't. But once she was gone, grief didn't give him anywhere else to go. He wanted to care, he wanted to do right, but something in him just wouldn't let him fucking do it.

I can say I genuinely had fun hunting that morning. We never did find that deer, and I had scars on my legs for a long while; but for once, sweet once, Dad meant well.

Seventeen

I called Mrs. Rodwell's sister, Clarice, from the landline at Katie's house when I got home from school. Cell phones existed, but I certainly didn't have one. Really, not many folks in Bellwether did yet. It wasn't like they were cheap back in those days, and no one in town was even sniffing rich—certainly no one in my circle of reach.

We'd set up an interview for Friday after school. *Interview* being a loose word; Clarice told me not to worry about it. It sounded like it would be all but a formality. I had never, to my knowledge, met Clarice, so I wasn't sure what to expect. Mrs. Rodwell was maybe in her midforties and looked . . . nondescript. She had brown hair and an Appalachian-looking face with hard but welcoming features—she could have been anyone in Bellwether. I wondered if her sister would be the same. I didn't even know if she was older or younger.

I rolled into the parking lot a few minutes after four o'clock. Based on the empty spaces I was pretty sure there weren't too many people checking in. Why would there be on a random Friday in Bellwether? I leaned my bike against the wall near the front entrance. No one was going to take it—there have to be people around for that to happen.

It was cold in the lobby. It smelled clean but still like a motel lobby: industrial cleaners; old coffee in the pot; carpets with weird patterns, cleaned in vain for years and years gone by.

There was an older-looking woman behind the front desk. Straggly graying hair, sun-scarred nose, dark brown eyes. She was wearing a denim shirt with the sleeves rolled up and a Motel 6 logo ironed on near the breast pocket. Fraying collars and wear patterns on the elbows. The shirt didn't look clean—like she'd been wearing it all week.

"Hi, I'm here to meet Clarice," I said when she didn't look up from her computer.

"You're looking at her." Her voice was loud and confident, brusque but sure. "Ah, good to meet you." She stood up and walked around the desk.

Clarice extended her hand well in advance of getting to me. Her shake was firm and her hands rough, calloused from manual labor—a blue-collar kind of woman. She was maybe half a foot shorter than me, a stout woman, but her presence was immediately larger than mine.

"Come, sit." She directed me over to a couch off to one side of the lobby and plopped into an adjacent chair. "So why do ya want to work at my hotel?"

"Well, Mrs. Rodwell said you were looking for help, and it sounded like a good opportunity," I explained.

"And I don't really have plans after graduating, so I guess I need to start figuring that out."

She smiled at me, rubbing her knees with her palms. I learned later that she struggled with arthritis, and her knees were almost always swollen. It didn't slow her down or stop her from working. She powered through no matter the pain; physical pain is nothing to injury of the soul.

"Well, that's fine," she said. "I'm happy to have you, but I can't be promisin' ya the most exciting work."

"That's okay," I said. "We all have to start somewhere." I tried a smile.

"That's right." She smiled with the right corner of her mouth and stood up and walked me back across the room. "Most of what you'll be doing is checking guests in and giving them room keys. Used to be we had a book but now everything is in a spreadsheet on this fucker." She patted the computer, a hunk of gray Dell technology. "I don't know how the hell to use it, that's why you're here."

"Okay," I said.

Unsurprisingly, I didn't have a computer of my own back then, but then again, not many people in town did. To say Bellwether was behind would be an understatement.

While computers in bigger towns were getting slimmer and faster, desktops like the one Clarice had were still downright fancy technology in Bellwether. Certainly, folks in town weren't going to be walking around with slim laptops like they were starting to in other places.

So it didn't come as much of a surprise to me that she didn't know how to use it—I hardly knew how to use it, and I was the generation that was supposed to learn. We had one typing class in school, on computers not dissimilar to the one at the motel. I knew how to type okay. I knew how to fill out a spreadsheet, and I knew how to access the internet. What more did I need?

Not much it turned out.

"Now," Clarice continued, "folks can make reservations online now. I don't like it, but they tell me it helps business, so guess I might should adapt. The login is on a sticky note under the keyboard in case you forget. Just copy over the reservations when they come in. It should be real easy for someone your age."

She wasn't wrong. It was all pretty straightforward—albeit tedious because she wanted everything in a single spreadsheet where she could print it to read and understand it. That made it hardly streamline, but it was the only way it made sense for Clarice.

"When can you start?" she asked when I didn't say anything.

We set my first shift for Monday after school. I only needed to work evenings because as Clarice explained, no one checks in in the mornings in Bellwether—they only get the hell out.

* * *

"Miss Jesse!" Mayor Wright was absolutely beaming as he walked into the office. "Do you have some time to chat after lunch? I want to tell you about some things we've been working on."

"Of course, sir." I felt a heat rise in my gut and knew I was blushing. Part of me worried I was in trouble, but the rest of me was able to read his mood.

I had been riding a high since Sheila's retirement party. Work had sort of returned to normal after a, relatively speaking, eventful few months. Having Sheila approve of Theodore made me feel better about seeing him, too, even though we still hadn't had the talk about what we were. Life was just going pretty darn well. It was hard, of course, as it always was in Bellwether, but a good hard—a positive and challenging hard.

I ate lunch at my desk and waited for Mayor Wright to call me into his office. Christina normally gave me a heads up if he was working on something important that I would have to field questions about, but she hadn't. Besides, it involved me, so it couldn't be that. As nice as he was, he didn't ask my opinions about the big things—why the hell would he?

"Jesse." Mayor Wright poked his head out of his office door a little after one, still sporting a big smile. "Ready?"

"Yes, sir." I nodded and stood up and followed him in.

I hadn't sat in Mayor Wright's office since I got hired. He meets with all of the new hires to get to know them, but after that I didn't have much reason to sit around in there. I had been in his office plenty, of course, such was the job, but I hadn't sat in the comfy leather chair across from his dark oak desk, only stood on the periphery.

"All right." He sat down and shuffled some papers, not losing the beaming grin. "Let me tell you what we're working with. Now, none of this is official, but based on the conversations I've had, I think we are going to have no problem at all getting it done."

I nodded to let him continue.

"I thought a lot about what we talked about with drug treatment versus enforcement," he continued. "I was actually able to get on a conference call with some advocacy groups and other small-town mayors to see what basic steps we can take to at least decrease the chances of folks dying from drugs.

"First, I'm going to ask the city council to allocate a portion of our annual budget to education and hopefully, knock on wood"—he knocked on his desk—"opening a new rehabilitation clinic in town. Now, that's a bit of a pipe dream, and we don't expect to have the funding any time soon, but it will never happen if we don't get that ball moving. How does that sound so far?"

"Um, incredible, sir," I offered. I couldn't help but smile. He had genuinely taken to heart the feedback I had given him. I knew he listened and cared and did so with everyone, but I never expected anything to come of it.

"Good." He smiled and continued, "Now in terms of what we are going to get into short term, I have been talking with folks on the city council, and this week we are going to pass a city ordinance requiring every government-owned building in town to stock a supply of naloxone, which is the drug used immediately after an overdose to save folks.

"It seems like a mighty simple thing, but a good thing, so I can't see why we shouldn't do that. We aren't encouraging folks to use but helping 'em out when they get themselves into trouble."

"Yes, sir," I said.

"Well, good," he said. "I just wanted to keep you in the loop on that. Christina will tell you when we know for sure, but it sounds like that'll be a done deal on Thursday, and we'll have something for me to sign that night. I, of course, would love for you to attend, if you don't mind."

"Of course, sir, it would be an honor."

I felt proud of my work for Mayor Wright most of the time, but that day I walked back to my desk with my shoulders back and my head held a little higher. I had a little more pep in my walk as I strode to my car when I got off work. I felt good; I had done good.

Theordore and I were having a night in at his apartment in the evening, the day I had my meeting with Mayor Wright. We had been spending more time together. Not like going out on formal dates, but just being around one another, living life adjacent to each other's presence.

We were sitting on the couch after dinner, watching a movie. I wasn't really paying attention.

"Guess what," I told him, sitting up to face him.

"What's up?" He turned to me.

"Mayor Wright took my input on something and actually changed his position!"

"Jesse!" He beamed at me. "No kidding? Good gracious, woman, that's fantastic!"

He gave me a big hug and asked me more about what we'd done and listened intently while I explained the full background of Mayor Wright asking my opinion in the first place, the interim when I didn't think anything would happen, then the meeting that day. In all my time with Jeff he'd never shown that much interest in my work—he had certainly never been that encouraging. I felt supported, and that was a special feeling.

Eighteen

"Want to go out to the house today?" I asked Katie as we biked to school. It was the most direct I had been in asking her in months—the first time I had said it aloud in longer.

My first day at the Motel 6 had been fine, mostly filling out tax paperwork then getting myself up to speed on the computer. It was simple, but there were intricacies I needed to learn, mostly driven by Clarice's own idiosyncrasies. Plus, being that it was a Monday, there were essentially no guests staying at the motel, either—the few weekend stragglers usually checked out early on Monday, trudging to the front desk looking worse for wear.

I had that Tuesday off—the plan was for the other front desk employee and me to switch off days until I graduated, then I would come on full time. There wasn't exactly enough work for the both of us, but Clarice said she just needed staff there. I already knew this plan would result in me cleaning more toilets than I'd signed up for, but I was getting paid a fair wage and didn't have to worry about finding a job after graduation, so I just accepted the role with gratitude.

I hadn't checked in with Katie in a while, though. Life had seemed like a whirlwind those few months—me trying to survive and Katie branching off with new friends in a world I didn't understand. We talked plenty, sure, but not about serious things. We talked about homework and cute boys and how the bike to school felt longer some mornings and the weather. We didn't talk about the directions of our lives.

It was May and we had been living together for just over a year, sharing a room that was close to too small for one person. As we grew apart emotionally, our metaphysical egos stole more space, and the bedroom felt far more cramped than it had when I moved in. It wasn't as though I was living with my best friend anymore; it was as though I was living with an adult person.

"Yeah, sure," she said. *Must not have plans with her other friends*, I thought.

She didn't seem particularly jazzed about going, but I didn't expect her to, if I was being honest. I frankly didn't expect her to go. I thought she would have plans with someone somewhere, and I wouldn't see her until after dinner. So I couldn't help but smile a little when she said yes. It felt like, I don't know . . . hope.

I followed a little behind Katie as we biked. Lately, I had begun to notice that she had changed physically. I mean, she still looked like Katie, but there was something different.

Her skin looked thinner and somehow a different kind of pale than it had always been, something more like a translucence from a vampire film. Her bright red hair had lost some vibrance, dulled, and seemed to have thinned, lost volume, and straggled down the sides of her face. It wasn't until we were biking that I really noticed the difference. It was striking.

As I rode behind her, I could see her backbones and ribs through the T-shirt she was wearing, even as it billowed in the wind. Her arms looked like rails reaching for her bike handles—like extensions of the metal frame itself—and her fingers had turned skeletal.

I didn't say anything. I wasn't sure what I would say. I loved Katie, but I wasn't ready to tell her I was worried about her. I would have to build up the courage. I knew that. I took a heavy breath and kept pedaling.

When we got up the hill, we parked our bikes outside of the house and checked to make sure no one else was there. We were alone, so we went inside and sat down leaning against the wall, trying to catch our breath and dry the sweat dripping from our brows. I noticed Katie was breathing harder than usual. We had been biking our whole lives. We'd covered about every inch of Bellwether together, and she was always more in shape than I was. Always. She had lungs for days and could pedal for hours without tiring.

This was the final cue. Something was bad; I couldn't deny it any longer.

"Katie, are you doing okay?"

"Uh, yeah." I felt her look at me, but I didn't turn to face her yet. "Why?"

"You look frail," I explained. I was still looking away, off into the forest through the window opposite us. I waved my hands aimlessly through the air searching for the words—for some guidance from the heavens to grab onto. Really, it didn't matter what I said. Any words would have been right—it was saying *something* that mattered. "I dunno, you just look off. I'm worried about you, Katie."

"Yeah, well, I'm fine." She sounded, if anything, defensive. She paused. She was scowling and looking straight ahead at nothing in particular. Perhaps she was looking at the demon in front of her, the one that had been lurking over her shoulder but was now out in the open for all to see. "Anyway, I gotta piss."

She stood up abruptly and walked outside. That conversation hadn't gone how I had hoped. I started to cry. I wasn't sure what to do. My cheeks burned, and my limbs felt numb. I was losing my best friend, and I was worried she was losing herself, too. I tried to steady myself, figuring she'd be back soon.

I stood up and walked a couple of laps around the interior of the house. I took big deep breaths. I remembered reading about square breathing and gave it my best shot. It didn't work, really. I was just too emotional. No air was getting in; no air was getting out.

I felt a pit in my gut when Katie didn't come back after a few minutes. Worried, I walked out of the house to look for her.

I found my best friend behind the one windowless wall of the house with a piece of plastic and coke straw. The plastic looked like something she had just found in the woods. It wasn't clean. I'm not sure she cared.

She looked up with her gaunt face and her expression didn't change much—almost like she couldn't even register that she had been caught doing something wrong.

She had already taken a line, and the look in her eyes disgusted me. She had never been particularly pretty, but she had once looked healthy. This version of Katie was a ghost—like her soul had died but forgot to tell her body. She didn't look eighteen, she looked forty.

"What the fuck," I said, not to her, but to the situation. I had no more words left to say. I had tried, and in the most tangible way I could imagine, I had failed.

I turned around, got on my bike, and pedaled away. I didn't pedal fast. I didn't scream or cry or slam my bike. I didn't get any cuts on my legs, and I hopped off to walk over the trestle. There was a finality in the air that demanded not belligerent anger but serene acceptance to the most abject grief.

Katie was gone. I was done.

I didn't want to go back to her house because I didn't think I could face her mom. I didn't know where else to go, so I went to the motel. I wasn't scheduled to work, but I had a feeling I wouldn't be turned away.

I'm sure I looked like hell, but I needed some place to be.

Clarice gave me a funny look when I walked into the lobby of the motel.

"Hot damn, is it Tuesday already?" she asked rhetorically. She pronounced her days without the *A*. *Tuesdy*. "What's going on, Jesse?"

I didn't know what to say; I hadn't planned that far ahead.

"I—I think I just lost my best friend, and—and well, I didn't know where else to go," I stammered. "I live with her, but I don't think I can even stand to look at her anymore."

"Well, you can stay here awhile, if you like." Clarice didn't interrogate me. She didn't make me feel bad. She just gave me a place to stay. I didn't need to think about taking her up on her offer. In my new room that night I wept alone and slept, from sheer exhaustion, sitting upright in bed.

Nineteen

The city council's meeting on Thursday was regularly scheduled for 7 p.m. I went occasionally, if Mayor Wright was speaking or needed me to take notes on something, but it was exceedingly rare that I was required to go. I certainly was never excited to go.

Small-town city council meetings are exciting sometimes, but most of the time they're pretty damn boring, to be honest—folks whining about stop signs and dog poop and things of the like. It wasn't sexy, but it was necessary. Someone had to do it, lest the whole town go to shit.

I worked a full day on the day of the first meeting I'd ever cared about, then went home to get ready. Normally, I would simply wear my normal work clothes to the meetings, but this one was special. Not only was Mayor Wright speaking, but I was there not in my capacity as an employee of the mayor, but as an Invited Guest of the Mayor. I wanted to look nice.

Christine had gotten word that morning to pass along to Mayor Wright that all of the council had made their decisions on which way they would go, and the vote would pass five to two. The two who were going to vote *no*, Ginny Pratt and Frederick Swann, were voting against the ordinance not because they really disagreed with it that much but mostly for symbolism, and because they could— they had only decided to vote against once they knew it would pass. The other five had freed them up to make a symbolic stand.

In fact, Fred told me privately later that he thought it was a good law, and he was proud Bellwether had enacted it. Irony. Even at the local level, politics is, invariably, political.

I only owned one pantsuit, and I literally never wore it. The dry-cleaning tag on it when I got it out that night was from two years before; that's how seldom I wore it. I only wore it on special occasions when I had a good excuse for it, and I figured this was as good as any.

It was deep black and looked, if I say so myself, pretty damn sharp. I paired it with a sky-blue blouse and a silver necklace that had belonged to Mom. I didn't wear jewelry that much, but a special occasion, this occasion, felt appropriate for such extravagances—and a way to honor Mom.

It was a freezing cold night, but the sky was a perfect black and was painted with stars. I felt some kind of alive when I got hit with the crisp breeze walking up the steps of city hall. In a movie there would've been cameras flashing and a crowd gathered for the big announcement—

instead I scared a squirrel away from the magnolia tree out front, and I was alone enough that I could hear its feet pitter on the cobblestone sidewalk.

When I walked into the chamber there weren't many people there. Staffers mostly, plus Janie Sanders. Janie was God knows how old. She attended every single city council meeting and spoke at every single city council meeting. She showed up every time, not to complain about anything or to ask questions, but to just sort of talk about whatever it was that was on her mind. It had become something of a tradition—it might as well have been officially built into the night's minutes.

Janie was there that night to talk about a particular herd of deer that had moved into her neighborhood. There was one young doe she found particularly cute. It was quite endearing to hear her describe in great detail how they eat the acorns from the big oak tree behind her house and how not everyone has an oak tree and how fortunate she was to have an oak tree because the deer came in real close to her back porch. It even got a smile from the local reporters who had to be there because they drew the short straw from their editor that night. It was small-town quaint to the nth degree.

Fortunately, Bellwether city council meetings, as a result of there not being particularly much to talk about on any given Thursday, were quite short. The minutes were read and agreed upon, there was some discussion on a sidewalk project which had been underway for a while—replacing cracked sidewalks with the aforementioned cobblestone—then Janie gave her usual talk, and then it was time to vote on the new law.

Because there had been so much discussion behind closed doors, it was largely procedural. One of the council members presented the proposed ordinance, they all voted on whether or not to allow debate—they voted not to debate, thankfully—then they had the vote.

I was surprised by how nervous I was when the moment came to vote. It was the moment of truth, after all. All of the hard work by people who weren't me was coming to fruition because I had told Mayor Wright I disagreed with him one time. There was no turning back; what was once a simple idea was becoming real life.

The vote was done by show of hands. Four needed to pass.

"The question is on the passage of the proposed ordinance."

I immediately saw three hands shoot up. I inhaled sharply. Then the fourth, then the fifth. Release.

I felt a firm hand on my shoulder. Mayor Wright had already stood up, knowing what the result would be. He smiled at me and motioned for me to stand up.

The chair declared the motion passed, signed it, and "formally" sent it to Mayor Wright for signature or veto. A table had been set up with a microphone in front of the chamber, as it always was if Mayor Wright was speaking or signing something.

The new town law—Bellwether Ord. 472 § 3, 2019—was placed on the table in front of him for signature, and he didn't hesitate. Then, to my surprise, he stood up and handed me the pen he used to sign it with.

"Never forget this night." He shook my hand and whispered in my ear, giving me a warm embrace. Then he turned to the reporters and the several people gathered in the room. "This is a good law—going to do a lot of good here in Bellwether" was his opening statement.

I appreciated that he let me maintain my anonymity. I didn't want the spotlight. I hadn't done any work for it. But I had provided the kernel of an idea, so it was special to be there. I was proud, real proud, that night.

Twenty

I still saw Katie at school after I moved out, but we never spoke. It was really sad and just didn't seem real. Her mom and dad had to help me move all of my stuff again. I think they understood—and I think that might have been the worst part of it all. They knew what was going wrong with their daughter, and they knew it had the potential to destroy me. too. But they didn't have the option to run away from it. They were in it. It was their own daughter, and they must have felt an almighty powerlessness to stop it. I couldn't imagine.

My life changed all because someone I hardly knew had said, *You can stay here if you want.* And I did. I finished classes without my best friend. I sat alone at graduation without my best friend, and I went out alone into the real world for the first time at eighteen years old.

I heard rumors that summer that Katie might have gotten into some heavier stuff. I heard she was making her money dealing—whatever money she might have had, that is. I heard she looked even worse than she had the last time we spoke, but I didn't know, I hadn't seen her. I didn't know if I even wanted to see her anymore.

I knew she wasn't living at home anymore. I had confirmed that much. But, really, since that day in the woods, I knew just about nothing for sure about her life. I didn't know who she lived with, who she hung out with, what parts of town she spent her time in. Nothing.

She had become an enigma, in the worst way possible. She was part myth, and the myth may have been the only reason she was still alive.

Until one day at work, I got a call: "Hello I'm calling for Jesse Strotherton."

"Speaking."

"This is Captain Voss from the Bellwether Police Department," the deep, not very southern voice on the other end of the line said. "I'm calling to see if you've seen or heard from your friend Katie lately."

"Um, no I haven't," I said, confused.

"Well, just give us a call if you do." He gave me his office number and hung up without letting me ask so much as a solitary question.

I got a pit in my stomach and told Clarice I needed to leave. She didn't question me; she could hear in my voice I meant it, and nothing was going to keep me at that motel. It was August, and it was scorching, but I didn't care as I hopped on my bike and hammered the pedals toward Katie's parents' house.

As I got close, I saw a car I didn't recognize in the driveway with a State Use Only plate. I saw Katie's mom in the yard talking to a man in a suit. They saw me as I saw them. I stopped on the road and balanced myself with one foot. We stared at each other for a moment before I realized what was happening. It felt like it happened in slow motion.

I got back on my bike and sprinted with everything I had to the one place I knew Katie might still be. The house.

I could feel the cop's car following me as I pedaled but I didn't give it any mind. I didn't hop off my bike at the trestle, though I nearly fell off. I didn't slow down until I saw Katie's bike, unmistakable, leaning against the outside of the house. It looked like it had been there awhile, rust dripping down its frame and mold starting to gather on its faux-leather seat.

I got off and called for Katie until my voice frayed. I yelled with every piece of my soul, but no one responded. I stepped toward the house, bounding with pounding steps through the weeds, and only then did I notice the smell.

I stepped to the doorway and saw what I feared: a little orange pill pottle, no lid, lying on the floor, pills scattered.

I stepped once more forward and saw a hand and a mop of strung-out red hair. The cop had made it up behind me. He was on foot, so it took him longer. He saw what I saw.

Cole William Barnhill

I thought about a rosary and a hotel room. Pooled blood and foam at the mouth. Broken corpses and lost souls.

"Oh God," he said. He was young—so young and naive he meant it. Soon enough, he'd get used to it. It comes with the job around these parts.

I got back on my bike and pedaled, softly this time, to Katie's house. I didn't know what I'd say. I knew there was nothing I could say that would brace what was coming.

There were more police cars out front when I approached. There must have been some kind of communication, but the key message hadn't been delivered yet. Her mom didn't know. I knew she didn't know—it would've been obvious.

Katie's mom must have been waiting for me because as soon as I pulled up, she opened the screen door. She stood there, holding it open with her foot, looking at me with a wistful, anticipatory expression. I had seen her in that position so many times before, poking her head out of the house to call us home for supper or to scold us for some kind of trouble we had gotten into. She never got real mad; she loved us too much for that. She loved Katie more than life itself. I wished, more than I'd ever wished before, this could've been one of those times.

I got off my bike and started walking through the lawn. It hadn't been mowed in a while—a sign of the burden Katie's turn had had on even her steel-faced father.

A heft settled on my chest. I tried to look away at first, but when Katie's mom adjusted her weight to her right foot, I knew she couldn't wait any longer. I couldn't hold it back, and I felt tears start to run down my face. I felt the grass sticking to the sweat on my legs and the hard beat of my heart coming through my chest.

I glanced to the sky, looking, hoping for a sign from God. It was a bright blue expanse. It had accepted Katie home.

I pursed my lips, looked her in the eyes, and shook my head.

There's no erasing that scream from your mind— no matter how many times you hear it. The young cop would never get used to that part. After so many deaths, I still hadn't.

Twenty-One

"Got plans tomorrow?" Theodore asked me over dinner one Friday.

"Not yet."

"Good," he said. "Let's go up to Roanoke and go to the mall."

"Do what now?"

"The mall," he insisted. "It'll be fun!"

Theodore never quite struck me as the mall-going type. I looked at him feeling suspicious of some ulterior motive for a moment. I was trying to figure out what his game was. There had to be a larger aim, but I didn't know what it was.

"Okay," I said. I wasn't going to say no to plans with him, anyway.

Valley West Mall was a nineties nostalgia trip. It smelled like perfume and candles and cheap American Chinese food and even cheaper pizza. Shoe stores and a wannabe-rebellious music shop, a cheap massage chair, and a guy trying to sell you a magic health drink. I'm not convinced people actually ever bought stuff there—save for old folks buying Christmas presents. But it was quaint, I liked that. I wish we all could go back to that.

I liked the food court. I loved a good food court, actually. I remember Katie's mom taking us to the mall once when we were kids. We couldn't afford to buy anything, of course, but it was a thrill to walk around and go into all the stores—looking at things rich people might buy. But the food court, oh baby, the food court. Katie and I shared a plate of orange chicken and fried rice. It was horrendous, I'm sure, but it was the greatest thing I'd ever tasted.

I guided Theodore by hand to that food court as soon as we got there. The food court is also a good place to gauge the vibe of the throng of weekend shoppers. There were, it should not have been a surprise, fewer people in the food court when Theodore and I walked in than there had been back in the day. Malls had faded in the internet age. That made sense, but it made me a little sad. Then again, there's really no sense in yearning for such a treacherous nostalgia.

The Chinese place in the left-hand corner was still there—or at least some version of it. I made a beeline in that direction.

Theodore humored me for lunch, as sadly, the flavor of the present day failed to live up to the memory of the past. I wouldn't say I was surprised. There weren't many people sitting in the food court with us. A few teenagers surely up to no good and some folks a little older than us who had nowhere better to be. None of them looked to be thoroughly enjoying their food.

"Okay, Teddy," I said after he cleared our plates. "What are we here for?"

"Why's there got to be a reason?" He winked but continued, "No, I know. This is, undisputed, the best place in the world to people watch. Folks up here are weird as hell, but they're 'bout as funny as can be to just sit down and watch."

The mall was laid out, more or less, as a crooked cross. One long main drag, bent at the bottom, with a shorter crossroad somewhere near the middle. The food court was near the intersection, but Theodore insisted the best people watching was at the point where the main thoroughfare turned.

We got ice cream—cookie dough for me, always—and he walked us down the off-white tile walkway to a little bench at the apex of the turn. From there, you could look to your left and see clear through to the north end of the mall and look to your right and see down the shorter way to the south end. There was, more or less, a clear view of most of the mall. A clear view to capitalistic reverie.

We sat and watched a group of high school–age boys puff out their chests and hope to impress some girls. Their khaki shorts were jacked up a little too high, and they wore their sweaty boat shoes without socks, which surely smelled ripe. Young kids being kids but doing it with money—something I hardly recognized.

Some giggling and red cheeks resulted in some bruised egos. Teen boys being teen boys with short memories and unending confidence, though, they moved on to the next gaggle of girls, hyping each other up to bust out the next well and truly horrid pickup line.

It was funny—and kind of sad. They strutted and strode up and down the mall for half an hour until they left, presumably to be picked up by a well-meaning parent.

There was a grandmother walking hand in hand with her pigtailed granddaughter. She shuffled, hunched over, with her big purse on one arm and the apple of her eye on the other. The little girl skipped along, bouncing with boundless energy but keeping the same, slow-but-steady pace of her shuffling matriarch. It made me reminisce on a time that never existed. I had hardly known my grandparents. Only two of them, Mom's parents, lived to see my birth. They both died young.

I looked over and Theodore was beaming, smiling at the grandmother-granddaughter pair. I grabbed his hand, and he circled his thumb on mine. He pointed down the way and chuckled.

A middle-aged businessman in a suit he couldn't afford was trying his luck with the twentysomething woman selling perfume at a middle-of-the-mall kiosk. She was stunning but in the way that was perfume-selling intentional. I can't imagine she actually did herself up like that in her day-to-day life. The things people do to pay the bills.

She played along with him, and he seemed sure he was in. She made the sale—he strutted away proudly. There was no chance they'd even see each other again, but they both won the conversation. It made me join Theodore in the chuckle.

"Want to walk?" he said after a while.

"Sure." I stood up. "Where to?"

"Let's go try on shit we can't afford." He grinned that grin. I laughed and followed.

As low as the mall may have fallen, its dingy walls and cracking exterior still housed, generously, a lot of shit we couldn't afford. Shoes were the first stop. Theodore tried on a few pairs of sneakers he could hardly afford to look at. He mimicked his basketball moves against an air defender, making it apparent why his playing days ended after middle school.

With some prodding I tried on an expensive pair of heels, and it turns out, just because they cost more did not mean they were any more comfortable. I looked ridiculous, like an early prototype of a humanoid robot whose legs weren't quite programmed right. I remembered why I never wore heels over an inch. High-dollar stilettos, while fabulous, simply weren't for me.

The teenage worker behind the counter at the shoe outlet looked on unamused and uninterested in our shenanigans. They didn't seem particularly disappointed when we politely put the shoes back on the shelf after trying them on. The less trouble the better when you're trying to get through your shift, I guess. Fair enough.

The shoe store was beside a wedding store—dresses, tuxes, ties of garish hues, gaudy bridesmaid wear, etc.—which I was, I admit, going to walk right on past. It looked snobbish, like there wouldn't be an employee inside who would welcome the likes of me in. I hadn't had a real wedding dress for my marriage to Jeff. Hell, my dress wasn't even white. It was off-yellow and hideous. I looked like I was going to the worst kind of prom, and my date had forgotten we were supposed to look nice—he hadn't even shaved.

"Let's go look." Theodore pulled me by the hand when we got near the entrance.

* * *

I still remember the only time I saw Mom's wedding dress. My folks didn't have pictures around the house from their wedding or anything. It was hard to even imagine what Mom had looked like young; most of the pictures we had were of my father. There were some of

Mom and me sprinkled in, but we weren't featured prominently.

I was playing hide and seek with Katie one time. I must have been maybe five at the time, young enough that I was still allowed to play in the house without fear of my father—not that that feeling lasted too long into my youth anyhow.

Katie was the one hiding, and I was tearing around the house looking for her. Room-to-room, all the usual places, I couldn't find her. We never went into my folks' room. Not that it was a rule, we just didn't. I didn't feel particularly comfortable in there, and Katie had plenty of hiding spots without it.

That day, though, Katie hid in their closet, way in the back, behind all of the clothes. I yanked the door open and swung back the hangers of bland blouses. Mom didn't have many clothes, and they weren't particularly flashy. In hindsight I think she might have liked to wear something more of a statement but was never able to while she was with my father.

In the back of the closet was Katie. I smiled in victory then stopped when I noticed the hidden gown. It was gorgeous, handmade by my grandmother with generous and classy lace accents. Floor length with an elegant train of the purest white. I was young, but I knew what a wedding dress was, and I knew what princesses looked like.

216

Mom must've looked like a princess in that dress. I never got to know. There may have been pictures, but I never saw them. Hidden away in something more than shame, Mom's dress became a mystery I never dared to solve. I never had my own dress and never learned what became of Mom's.

I wished she'd had a better wedding. I wished I'd had a better dress. It doesn't matter—it's not what you're in, it's who you're with. In that regard, neither of us had what we needed, only what we thought we deserved.

* * *

The inside of the wedding store was wall-to-wall formal wear. Men's to the right and women's to the left. Nearly as far as the eye could see, the most stunning dresses in every color I could image and then some. The dresses lined the racks, lined the walls, lined every nook and cranny. Then to the back, a sea, pure and deep, like an inviting abyss, all of the stunning white wedding gowns I could dream of.

I hid a grin, but only a little. I pulled Theodore the other way. If we were going to go in there, I was going to make the man put on a tux.

I strolled along the racks of tuxedoes fingering the varying colors and fabrics as I went. I winked at Theodore. "Hmm, what do we think would look best on you?" I poked at him, flipping through garishly bright hues of exuberant clothing.

He smiled, walking a stride behind me with his hands in his pockets. He shrugged in a coy sort of way as I stopped at the magnificent section of blues.

"How about this?" I pulled out a gorgeous, sky-blue tuxedo.

Theodore laughed. "Only one way to find out."

I waved down an employee whose expression allowed us only ambivalence at best. She walked over with an employer-required sense of urgency. The woman had evidently dyed black hair with classy hoop earrings and subtle red lipstick. She was objectively beautiful, and she wore her black slacks and blouse in a way that told me she didn't come from money, which made me respect her a little.

Amanda, so said her nametag, took Theodore's measurements and whisked away into the apparently cavernous storeroom to find the right size. It didn't take her long to find it.

I wandered around a bit as he went into the Superman phone booth–style changing room, feeling the ever-watching eye of Amanda. If I could tell she didn't come from money, I knew she could tell that I came from poor. I would've bet all the money to my name that she had instructions to look out for folks like me stealing things we really couldn't afford.

Not that I, strictly speaking, couldn't afford a nice outfit on my government salary—I had mostly been conditioned away from even considering spending that sort of money, I guess. Big money is still big money to someone who grew up poor, no matter what changes they might go through.

Theodore strolled out of the changing room looking like a vintage of another era and a separate make. The blue suit pants made his legs look miles long, and wearing such a pristine tuxedo with his old brown boots was humorous, but it worked. Maybe it wouldn't have for anyone else, but for him it did.

"Okay, I did my part." He smirked at me. "You're turn to pay up, Jess."

I rolled my eyes and felt the warmth of blush in my cheeks. I didn't want to admit it, but I was excited, almost eager, to try on a wedding dress. Not that I wanted to get married or had even thought about it regarding Theodore. It was the freedom—the ability to have a white wedding dress if I wanted to.

"Okay, Unabomber." Amanda gave me a weird look. I suppose that's not a particularly normal thing to say out loud. "You have to pick, though." I grabbed him by his lapels and kissed him on the cheek. He damn near skipped over to the dress side of the store, like a kid in a candy shop.

The dresses were organized by color, then by size. He went for the whites, and I showed him to what had once been my size—back when I knew what size dress I wore, anyhow.

I sort of expected Theodore to find the most outlandish dress he could. There were plenty of absurd dresses with levels of poof that shouldn't be seen at a dance recital, much less a wedding. Dresses with unreasonable jeweling. Dresses which were too short to possibly say *classy*. Any dress you could imagine, any hideous dress you could dream of, they had them among the gems.

But he didn't go for one of those. He took his time. He walked from one end of the row to the other, carefully examining every dress. Toward the far right of the rack, near the back of the store, he stopped. He ran his fingers up and down the front of one of the dresses, turned it over in his hands, examining every stitch and every hem—every decision made by the designer. He had a focus in his eyes, and his tongue pressed into his cheek in thought.

Then he smiled and took the dress from the rack.

"This is the one." He grinned that grin at me. My cheeks felt warm again.

"Oookay," I said, feigning coy. If Amanda could see through it, which she clearly did, then surely so did Theodore.

I went back to my own phone booth–sized changing room and found myself nervous as I undressed.

I wasn't sure whether the dress would fit, it had been a long while since I bought a dress and wasn't completely sure what size I ought to wear. I felt something like a phony— as if the world knew I wasn't the kind of person born to be putting on a dress this nice in a room like this for a man like Theodore. I was an impostor who hadn't been outed but for whom the consequences of this charade would be dire.

A fraud like me can't keep up the facade for long. I thought maybe I should leave, but I didn't. Something in my soul kept me stuck there in that room with that dress. Something wasn't letting me exit the circumstance I found myself in, no matter how much I didn't think I deserved it.

I slid the dress on, and it seemed right. Better than right. I peeked my head out and whispered to Amanda to help with the zipper, which she cordially obliged.

"Like a glove," she said, patting me on the shoulders after doing up the zipper. It was a sleeved dress, understated silk with a bit of lace around the middle and a short train. I never would have picked it out myself, but it fit wonderfully and was, regardless of taste, quite a nice piece of clothing.

I looked down at the unbelievable glacial-white material hugging my body down to my bare feet. I wiggled my toes on the gray speckled carpet and confirmed they were mine. I grazed the silk along my waist, it felt cool and soft and sat on my skin without a crease, as if it ought to be there. My fingers liked the way the dress felt, the way my hips felt under their touch. The body was mine. The dress was real, and it was fabulous. I took a deep breath and smiled.

"Oh my lord" was all Theodore said when I walked out. I spun around, looking at myself in the mirror, looking at his reflection looking at me.

I felt a new sensation tumbling around in my soul. I'd never felt that before. It was the first time I understood the saying about butterflies in my stomach, and I could've sworn I saw a tear in Theodore's eyes, too.

Twenty-Two

"Miss Jesse."

"Bill!" I perked up from my work at that old familiar baritone.

"Do you have a moment for me?" Bill looked, enough so that I noticed, tired. He looked like himself—still cheerful, still well dressed, still proud shoulders, and a gleam in his eyes. But tired.

"For you? Always!" I said. "Let's go." I stood up and gave him a big hug then walked with him to grab a coffee.

We sat across from each other in the staff kitchen like we had so many times before. Bill shuffled around pouring coffee from the always-full pot into a pair of porcelain mugs from the cabinet. In addition to our personal mugs, there was a set of uniformly designed white mugs which mostly got used at official meetings or when personal mugs were dirty—I wondered sometimes if each mayor had their own design, but probably not.

"What's on your mind, Bill?" I smiled as I blew on my steaming coffee.

"Oh, nothing too much," he said a little too wistfully to be honest. "I just haven't gotten to check in with you in a while. What's new in your life, dear?"

My mind went to Theodore and the fact I hadn't told Bill a whole hell of a lot about him. There was a lot more to say, as it had been a while since we'd chatted about it.

"Well, I'm still seeing Theodore. It's been . . . gosh I guess it's been a little while now." I stumbled a bit.

Bill had a special kind of glimmer in his eye as I talked.

"Oh good, Jesse," he said. He reached out and squeezed my hands. Even in his climbing age his hands were strong, like a father's ought to feel. "Good."

"Yeah." I felt a blush and smiled to myself more than Bill. "It's been really good. I, uh, I really enjoy spending time with him, I guess."

"Jesse . . ." I could see Bill turning language over in his mind to choose the right words. "Dear, in thirty seconds across two days, you've told me more about this fellow than you've ever told me about anyone else."

I hadn't said all that much out loud, but I knew what he meant. Bill continued.

"Dear, I think it's time you say out loud the thing you've been avoiding." He smiled heartily into my eyes. "This fellow isn't Jeff . . . It's okay."

Huh. I chuckled a little to myself, finally letting myself admit it.

"Wow," I said. "Bill, I love him." I smiled and laughed. "Why didn't you tell me!"

I jokingly prodded him on the arm.

"You have to come to that feeling yourself, dear," he said. "You absolutely have to come to it yourself."

I smiled into my coffee and took a long sip. It tasted a little better than I had remembered. I wondered if it was a different brew.

Bill sat quietly for a moment. He was looking at me, still with a slight smile. I wasn't looking at him; I was still looking down. I felt an odd feeling, not necessarily joy—but then again, I'm not sure there was a word for what I felt.

What I could describe was that I felt Bill shift in his seat. It was a nervous kind of shift. I could feel that. I looked up at him, trying to give him tacit permission to say what was on his mind—and there was clearly something on his mind.

"Jesse, I've got something to tell you." He hesitated, tracing the rim of his mug. "I don't want you to hate me for it."

I smiled and returned the favor, taking my turn to grab his hand in reassurance. "Bill, why would I ever be mad at you?"

"I don't know, dear." He smiled and half chuckled. A visible release washed over him. "Well, there's no easy way to tell you, but I'm officially retiring. I'm calling it a career. Effective the last of the month."

I smiled and stood up and gave Bill, still seated, a gentle hug.

"Why in tarnation would I be mad at you for that, sir?" I sat back down across from him. "That's wonderful news. You deserve it."

"Well, thank you dear," he said. "It's probably past time. I'm sure I've been quite the drag around here, but I just don't think I was ready." He pursed his lips for a moment then exhaled deeply. "Well, I am now—'course I had a little poking from Cathy-Anne to help me along. It's time for this old fart to hang it up. We've already got a week scheduled to go see all the grandbabies after I'm done."

I was plainly happy for Bill. I knew I would miss seeing him at work, and I would miss taking breaks and drinking coffee with him. But the man had put in his time. He had raised a family and served them well for his entire adult life.

He deserved a chance to spend time—good quality time—with Cathy-Anne and to go and visit the kids for once. Coming to visit Bellwether is only so much fun, and their children lived in, objectively, nicer places to visit.

It was time for Bill to go where he wanted and do what he wanted. The love of a grandparent knows no bounds, and I was so happy Bill was going to get the chance to truly let that love reign.

* * *

"When did they start wrapping hay bales in plastic? Seems a waste, don't you think?" Theodore and I were back in the bed of his truck, looking out over the farm.

I had been the one to suggest the date this time. I'd wanted a romantic night with Theodore, away from other people, and the weather was just too nice to stay inside.

"What?!" I laughed out loud. The comment was out of the blue and such a preposterously funny thing to say.

"I don't know." He shrugged coyly. "Just seems like they're all plastic now. I remember when the old farmers used damn natural fiber ropes to hold 'em together. These young guys, all this equipment, they're just lookin' for a goddamn shortcut. That's not the point of farming— hell, that ain't the point of hay!"

"You tell 'em Teddy." I elbowed him in the side and punched my fist sarcastically. He laughed and grinned that grin at me, and I kissed him on the cheek. He was illuminated pink and blue by the setting sun and looked awfully handsome. Goofy. But handsome.

"Anyway . . ." He was still smiling and let out a hearty, deep breath. "Do you ever think about getting remarried?"

I blushed hard. I mean, my cheeks must have been tomato red. Store bought, not heirloom. Deep heat behind my face. The question was as out of the blue as his hay bale comment.

"Umm . . ."

"Not to me." He quickly deflected. "Just in general."

"Um, well . . ." I searched hard for the diplomatic words. "I didn't used to, but I guess I kind of do sometimes now . . . I guess."

I waited for the instant it took him to respond with an awful sort of bated breath.

"Well, damn, ain't that something," he said with his grin growing even more sly. "I do too, sometimes." He added with a wink, "I guess."

"Something, indeed." I gave him another kiss. "Can't say I ever thought I'd be thinking about it again after Jeff, and I can't say I wanted to."

"Ain't that the truth. It all came to an end so quickly. Shoot, I guess I just never thought I would get the chance to feel that way again," he said. "Certainly not any time soon, y'know."

"Yeah."

"I mean, after she left there were some bad nights, some real bad nights." I let him continue to wander with his words. He had those sorts of honest moments sometimes. I think they were good for him, and they taught me things about him I would never know otherwise. "But now, I just don't have 'em so much anymore. I miss how I felt about her, I suppose. But hell, I hardly even feel that anymore. Things are just good now, y'know."

"Yeah."

"I mean, I loved Mary, but I didn't love her how I feel now—"

"Um, what?" I interjected.

"Hot damn, I guess I hadn't told you that yet." He sat up a little and earned the brightness in his eyes. "I love you, Jesse."

I had never really told Jeff that I loved him. I had never said those words growing up—it's just not how we were in my family, for better or worse. It was always *Love ya,* not the three-word phrase that means something more.

It took a long time and a kick in the pants from Bill, but I finally said the words I'd never understood—the words I'd wanted to know my whole life.

"I love you, too, Unabomber."

Twenty-Three

I never told anyone about it, but I actually saw Katie one last time after I moved out of her house. I tried to forget, honestly. I really did. I didn't want to remember my friend like that.

It was at the grocery store late one afternoon in the middle of July, and I was picking up some snacks for my room. I ate most of my meals at the motel from the food we had available for guests, but I always afforded myself some junk to keep stocked in my room. A girl gets hungry, and motel food isn't an everyday kind of diet.

To be frank, I didn't even recognize Katie at first. I could've been convinced it was a zombie walking up in front of me. Her clothes were far too big for her by that point—tattered, too. Gray sweatpants and an unrecognizable Bellwether High School T-shirt draped loosely over her tiny, bony shoulders. Her shoes had laces, but over her skeletal feet they seemed to serve the shoes no true purpose as they had been wrenched as tight as they could go and still had give. I'm not sure what kept them on her feet other than the sullied shuffle of her walk. She was a shell of the form I'd once known.

She noticed me before I knew it was her. Say what you will, she never lost her outgoing nature or her ability to recognize a face, no matter how far gone she was.

"Jesse," she said, trying a smile on her gaunt, wax paper–thin face. She reminded me of pictures I'd seen of soldiers before and after a war—they were changed, the same person, but in so many ways, not. She certainly didn't look eighteen anymore. She didn't have anything in her shopping cart, and I couldn't imagine what she might be buying. Food for her and her parents, I hoped, but I was probably wrong.

"Good God, I never thought I'd see you again." She tried again to smile, but in vain. It looked like she'd lost a few molars—eaten by cavities, perhaps.

"Yeah," I said, looking for a neutral inflection. "Same."

"Do you have a minute?" she asked. There was a stark desperation in her voice.

"Yeah, I do."

I left my cart at the end of the aisle. If someone moved it, I'd take it as a sign that today wasn't a grocery day. We went to sit together in the café at the front of the store.

We were the only ones there, save for the bored employee whom I recognized as a sophomore girl from the high school but whose name I didn't know. We greeted the girl mutely, and I let Katie buy me a small coffee with a handful of coins she pulled from her pocketbook. I had seen people count out the exact change from loose change before, but it hurt to see Katie do it.

"So what are you up to now?" she asked when we sat down. She took the lid off her coffee and poured a little too much sugar into it.

"I'm still over at the motel," I said.

"Right, yeah, I forgot," she said and looked out the window to her left. "How's that?"

"It's not sexy, but it's steady work, I guess."

"Yeah . . ." She took a scalding sip of coffee. "Yeah, I get that."

I let the silence hover over us for a moment. It was awful, but I didn't know what to say. I didn't feel a present-day connection with the skeleton of a human sitting in front of me. It was like I was looking at a time-reduced memory of what I thought Katie had looked like but just couldn't remember that well. All of the life had been lost— in memory and in time.

I didn't want to pity her. I wanted to remember her as she was. Just as I was letting myself drift off into a charmless morose, Katie changed the subject.

"Did you hear what happened to Jimi?" she asked. "You remember Jimi, right? I think you and him hung around together a couple times. Over at the old house. Tall guy, thin, knows everything about every album ever released—well, knew, I guess."

"Um, I think so." The name sounded familiar, but I didn't connect the dots until later. She sounded something adjacent to excited to have juicy gossip for me. "What about him?"

"He got shot." Katie punctuated the sentence with a staccato *T*, leaning in across the table to tell me with vigor.

"Um, what?" I was taken aback. Of all the directions I had thought that story might go, that was not the one.

"Yeah," she said, falling over herself to get to the next part of the story. I had heard that tone in her voice so many times. Her brain always worked faster than her mouth would take it. She always had ideas a step ahead of her capacity to explain them. "He went to his guy to get some crank—Jimi got way into the heavy stuff. Like, so far in. No path out kind of deep into it. Total tweaker, Jimi. Anyway, he shows up without any cash and tries to pull a fast one. His guy tells him 'No, you gotta pay. I don't care if you're a loyal customer.'

"Jimi tells him 'Fuck off. Pass me the fucking balloon. You know I'm good for it.' Dealer isn't having it, though, and pulls out a .45 and pops him once in the chest and just stands there as Jimi bleeds out. Awful scene. Cops rocked up 'cause someone heard the shot. Open-and-shut. Dealer goes to prison. Crazy stuff."

"Wow," I said. I'm not sure there was a good way to react to that story. "That's intense."

"Yeah," Katie said. "Just bad news all around."

"So what are you up to?" I asked. I had to allow her the space.

"Oh . . ." Her voice sounded weak, strained, tired. "You know, just floating around."

She let a heinous silence overwhelm us. I thought I might have seen a lonesome tear make the old college try in her eye, but it just couldn't come out. That arrow just wasn't in her quiver anymore.

I didn't know if she was even still living at her folks anymore at that point. I know they moved out of the house not long after she died. They're still alive, last I'd heard. They finally got out of Bellwether. They had to. There was too much there, too much pain, too much rot. Too much there to keep grieving parents alive.

"Yeah." I tried to sound reassuring, not judgmental. I don't know how successful I was. I wanted to ease the burden for her. I could see she didn't know how to answer the question much more than I knew how to ask it. "It's hard out there for sure," I conceded.

"Yeah," she said. She half smiled and chuckled. "Yeah, it really is . . . Anyway, I should let you get back to shopping."

"Okay."

"It was really great to see you, though," she said, sitting up in her chair. "Hopefully next time it won't be so long."

"Yeah, it was great to see you, too." I heard the wistful tone in my own voice.

I stood up and hesitated to walk away, but I felt a new energy in Katie. Something moved in her, and her hand shot up to my arm. She squeezed my forearm with everything she had left.

"Jesse." She looked me square in my fucking eyes, deadly earnest. "Don't ever touch this stuff. Please . . . Don't ever touch this stuff."

I knew what she meant. A month later she was dead.

* * *

"So what really happened with you and Mary?" I asked Theodore in the car on the way home. Zoning out from the music as we rode, I realized I had never gotten the full picture. I just knew it had been harder for him than my divorce was with Jeff—his love had been purer.

He hesitated, scratching his chin as if he wasn't sure whether to tell the truth or not.

"Really," he said slowly, "I was doing a lot of drugs at that time—like anything I could get my hands on. She probably wasn't wrong; I was out of control but . . . I don't know, it's all sort of a blur, but she left, and I don't even know that I was really aware that she was leaving."

"When did this all happen?" I asked, knowing the answer but wanting to hear him say it.

"Oh, a couple months back, maybe." He was deflecting.

"So right when we met?" I got to the point.

"Yeah, I guess."

"So when we met, you were using anything you could get your hands on?"

"Yeah, I guess that's right," he conceded, looking guilty in a way I hadn't meant to make him feel.

But still, I was angry that my gut had been right. He'd been using, and the little things I had noticed—the changes in his energy, the messing with his nose at the bar, the jitters and jumps— had all been signs that I had chosen to ignore.

I'd been down that road before, and I knew how dark it got. I'd lost people I cared about—people I'd loved. I'd seen communities stricken by drugs—by that godforsaken epidemic that swept through Appalachia. From my high school, at least ten people from my graduating class had died.

Good people struck down. Good people killed. Not that it was in my face all the time, but it was always there, always lurking.

I felt, fair or not, justified in my disgust in learning Theodore's drug use was not, in fact, an old habit but something more present. It was a beast in the room with us still that I now found myself forced to contend with.

"Okay." I let him out of it. For now.

I was angry, but rage can kill a relationship—and I loved him too much for that. I had learned lessons and wanted to tread more carefully this time. Anger in love is different from anger in indifference—I learned that lesson the hard way.

I didn't call Theodore the next day, though. I just couldn't find a way to do it. I needed a moment, an ellipsis in our day-to-day lives, to slow down while I gathered my emotions. I didn't want my feelings to be too raw the next time we talked. And I wasn't even sure if I really believed I was in the right.

I didn't call him the day after, either. I probably should have. But I wasn't ready.

By the next day something had shifted in me. Something in the breeze brought into my soul a calm resolution: my love for Theodore was too large to let any obstacle stand in our way.

It was a normal Monday morning in Mayor Wright's office. The weather was fine. Not great, but fine.

I wasn't tired, but happy. I walked into city hall with new clarity and purpose. I suppose love does that to you.

It was the time of year when things just weren't all that busy around the mayor's office. City council had about wrapped up their work for the year, but it wasn't quite to the holiday season yet. It was an awkward sort of in-between in which Mayor Wright was the solitary piece of glue holding Bellwether together, regardless of whether or not it would fall apart if he weren't there, anyway—and it wouldn't have.

I was trying to make myself busy transcribing data into a spreadsheet, but that's not particularly important. It was a warmer day, so I'd worn a short-sleeve blouse under my winter coat and felt warm even in that. In the heated office it was even worse.

In lieu of coffee, I was drinking a tall glass of ice water. The water in city hall had an odd taste—not bad, exactly, but it certainly didn't taste like purified water. That flavor is engrained in my brain. The memory of a major event will do that to you.

I remember hearing a general shuffling coming from the area of Mayor Wright's office. Not that that was abnormal, but things sounded a bit more chaotic than what I considered usual. I figured, as always, that Christina or Mayor Wright would come and get me if I was needed, so I didn't go back there. I tried not to intrude, as a general rule, and I think that was usually for the better. I never really missed the important stuff, as far as I knew.

A little past noon I heard whispering behind the door that lead to Christina's desk and Mayor Wright's office. It was hurried, nervous sounding, but I couldn't make it out. Then it died down. The door was made of thick, sound-muffling oak, so the fact that I was able to discern any talking at all was abnormal.

A few minutes later the door opened to a crack. It didn't open the rest of the way, as if whoever was on the other side was finishing up a conversation—but there was no talking that I could hear. It dawned on me that whoever opened the door might be steadying themself, gathering themself, readying.

I figured someone from the state government or some town elder had died or something of the sort. Another old bastard to be forced to mourn even though we didn't mean it. I expected it to be Christina coming to give me the bad news and that she was taking a moment because it might have been someone she knew—it might be personal to her.

But it was Mayor Wright.

He walked over and pulled a chair over to the side of my desk and sat down. In all my time there he had never done this. Never.

He scooted in, elbows on my desk. His sleeves were rolled up and wrinkled. He looked closer to disheveled than I'd ever seen him. He spoke softly, leaning his head in, shrinking the space between us to talk to me directly.

"Jesse," he said. "I just got a phone call." He paused and pursed his lips. I couldn't tell if he was trying to compose himself or to find the right words—probably both. "Your friend, Theodore . . . He was found unresponsive in the bathroom of the bar where he works."

I felt all of the blood drain from my face, betraying my attempt to steady my expression. I let Mayor Wright fight through the pause. He was dead. I fucking knew he was dead.

"He had a pulse," Mayor Wright explained. "It was faint, but it was there. They administered naloxone, and he was rushed to the hospital. Jesse . . ." He put his hand on my arm. He'd never done that before. "He's okay." He leaned down to look me square in the eyes and make sure I heard him and make sure I listened. "I'm going to have Christina take you to the hospital to see him."

I had stopped listening after *he's okay*. Well, not stopped listening, exactly. I couldn't hear Mayor Wright anymore. I can't even describe the feeling—I don't think anyone can explain it without experiencing it themselves. I was weeping in a sort of uncontrollable way I would have thought only existed in movies if I hadn't seen it done before. I felt as though every tear I'd ever produced and ever could produce was pouring from my eyes. It was like every emotion I had felt, every pain I had held in for thirty-one years was being expelled at once from deep within me.

I stood up when Mayor Wright did, not because I knew what was happening, but because something in my bones made me do it. I don't remember getting into the car or the drive to the hospital.

I do remember what Christina said to me as we walked through the doors of the hospital.

"Jesse," she said into the distance. She wanted me to know what she was going to tell me, but she couldn't bear to look right at me when she said it. "You know, I lost my sister to an overdose. In 1979. She was only fifteen. I was in the next room, Jesse. I felt so guilty. And there wasn't . . . You know, there wasn't any way to save someone back then.

"I knew she had been using drugs, but I didn't say anything. I could see it in her face that she needed help, but I wasn't there for her. I wish I had been, looking back. It started out with pills after surgery, and she just couldn't stop. She kept finding ways to get more, and one day she took too many, and it killed her. Our mom found her. Goodness, it was awful.

"Anyway, I would do anything to take that day back. I wish there was some way . . ." She took a breath. "I wish there was some way to help back then, but there just wasn't, dear.

"All of this is to say, you've done a lot of good, Jesse. Getting Mayor Wright to consider that program was a good thing, and them getting it done was a really good thing. I wish we had had it back then, but if it can save lives now, then I think my sister can rest just a little bit easier. And it has.

"What I mean to say is that it can hit anyone. He's a good man, Jesse, and this isn't a flaw in him. It's a disease. And I can't tell you how to feel, but I can tell you what I know. He doesn't need your anger in him using drugs or your judgment, wishing he'd gotten clean. He needs your love right now."

Tears flowed more than they had before as she spoke. I knew she was right. It was true; Theodore needed me to love him. I knew from losing Katie—from the scars of the past—that he wasn't going to be healed in one day by my love, but it would only get worse if I abandoned him. If I left, then there'd be no bringing him back until he was being carried down the mountain from an abandoned house in a body bag.

Bellwether Hospital was not, and is not, what you're probably picturing. Or maybe it is. Two floors of gray walls with a too-dim lobby and two hallways extending out in either direction on the top floor. ORs were downstairs, so was the ICU. Everything else from deliveries to hospice to kids with broken legs was on the second floor.

It made for a strange environment. Hope and sorrow and triviality neighbored each other on a day-to-day basis. It must have been an odd experience for the doctors and nurses who labored so many hours in that wretched place.

It was quiet when we walked into the lobby. The quiet whisper of TVs playing Fox News and the deep snore of the man in the corner who couldn't keep his eyes open anymore. Good news was coming for him, I hoped.

"We're here to see Mr. Theodore Townes," Christina told the woman behind the desk when we walked in. I was still in a bit of a daze, so she continued to lead for me.

"Ah, yes ma'am. Mayor Wright called and told us you'd be coming over." The woman stood up and smiled. "He's in room 217, upstairs to the right."

"Thank you very much." Christina nodded and put her hand on my back to lead me forward. She moved her hand up and down my back in a reassuring gesture.

It made me feel important, having the mayor call ahead for us. It dawned on me for the first time that I didn't know how they'd even known to call Mayor Wright's office in the first place. But at that point, I didn't really care.

I was glad they had, and I was worried about Theodore, sure that I'd see a withering heap of a man in his room, intubated and clinging to life.

I was wrong.

"Jesse Strotherton as I live and breathe!" Theodore's voice got to me before I even processed him. I'm sure my countenance was not reassuring.

Theodore was sitting up in his bed, wearing a T-shirt and well-worn jeans instead of a hospital gown. He looked, perhaps, a bit tired, but most distinctly, he looked like himself. He was flipping through channels on the TV but turned it off when I walked in.

"You're alive?" It came out as a question. I wasn't surprised at him being alive—I knew that already—it was that he was so alive.

"Honey, they can't kill me that easy." He winked at me and waved me into the room.

"I'll leave you two alone," Christina said and turned to go back downstairs.

Twenty-Four

"What the hell happened?" I asked Theodore as I sat on the edge of the hospital bed beside him.

"Well . . . I didn't want to admit it, for a whole lot of reasons, but I guess my problem never went away. I didn't used to do drugs—I swear to everything—but ol' Jack started giving me stuff, and I guess I was pretty down. I think Mary leaving made it worse, which is kind of ironic when you think about it.

"I tried to stop, though, honest, when I met you. Well, not right when we met but once I knew I wanted to be with you forever— and I knew that I wanted my forever to be longer than a couple of weeks and an OD.

"I know I shouldn't have, but I suppose I've got real bad impulse control, and I got the urge last night towards the end of my shift—must've been almost four in the morning. I get into that dark place, and the late nights make it worse, I know it. But a man's got to work, and I'm not qualified to do a whole lot.

"Anyway, I tried, but . . ." He looks as though he might cry. "I just couldn't shake myself out of it.

"I went into the bathroom and took a bump. Shit wasn't clean, obviously, and I went down like a goddamn sack. I don't really remember what happened after that. Might be that I was dead for a while, I don't know—I didn't see God or anything like that if that's what you're thinking. But next thing I knew I was sitting here, and they were telling me how damn lucky I was."

I paused for a moment after he stopped talking. I wanted to make sure he was done, to give him the space to say what he needed.

"Wow" was probably not what I should have said. It was better than saying something judgmental, though, I guess. "So how long do you have to stay here?"

"Oh, not too long now!" He smiled, a thankful smile if anything. "They said they just want to keep me around 'til about lunch time just to be safe. Most folks who survive an overdose are out of the hospital in about an hour, sometimes a little more, once their vitals are normal. Naloxone is wild stuff, I tell you what."

"Wait, wait, wait," I said, backtracking his story in my head. "I'm missing something here. What happened after you almost fucking died?"

"Oh, well, that's the thing," he explained. "They had to tell me what happened 'cause obviously I didn't know, being half-dead and whatnot."

"I see that."

"Apparently someone heard me fall, and it turns out, me bragging on you pays off 'cause my colleague Frank had heard that they put naloxone in all the government buildings because some woman who works down at city hall kept bugging Mayor Wright until he did something."

"I didn't—"

"I know, but that's not how I told the story." He smirked. "You're real persistent in my version of the tale. Anyway, because I had told everybody and their brother about that talking about you, ol' Frank ran down to the post office 'cause it was only a block away.

"Long story short, he may have broken into the post office, but the cops told him not to worry about it because he grabbed the meds from the container in the lobby and hauled tail back to the bar.

"Took them two doses to get me back to life, but by the time the paramedics showed up my vitals were just about fine—or at least what they tell me. I don't know on account of being goddamn out of it." He paused. "Not saying you saved my life but . . ." he winked again.

"Ha, I didn't do a thing." I didn't hide my smile but let it fade. "Theodore . . . You are the one who did this to yourself, though."

I found myself frustrated with Theodore but struggling with it. I didn't want to be upset with him, but I was. But I also loved him, and he needed love in that moment.

"I know," he said. He looked away from me, and I saw something like shame creep into his eyes. I hated that for him. "I wish I could take back the first time I used and never do it again, but I can't. It was wrong then, and it was wrong last night. Hell, I was just lucky before now. Lucky last night, too, I suppose."

"Really damn lucky," I said and grabbed his hand. He had to know I still loved him. I had to make sure he knew. It was time to give him that love and to grant him grace.

"You know, they almost got me once." I started. "The opioids. I was really, really young, maybe five or six. Anyway, I'd broken my arm on the playground. It broke pretty bad and did some stuff to my nerves, so I was in a world of pain.

"Well, my father, piece of shit he was, gets unceremoniously told by Mom that he's got to take me to the doctor. Doc gets me fixed up enough, bones back in place and the works. I get a cast and a prescription.

"Well, it turns out this moron of a doctor wasn't much brighter than my father and gave my prekindergarten self a prescription for some high-strength opioid—oxy, maybe. A low dose, but still, not something I needed to be taking. Mind you, this is back when that stuff was brand new and triplicate prescriptions weren't even a thought yet.

"So we go to the pharmacy to pick the stuff up, and they tell my father the price. I don't remember how much it was, but we certainly didn't have insurance, so my father basically tells the pharmacist to fuck off and tells me I'll be fine with aspirin.

"A painful couple of months later and I got my cast off. I was angry at my father then because it hurt, and I felt like I shouldn't have to be in pain just because my father was cheap—or seemed cheap to my young brain. But looking back, that might have well been what saved my life, you know. Who knows, maybe I'm wrong, and maybe I'm overthinking it. But maybe I would've gotten addicted. Maybe my fate and Katie's would've been reversed. And maybe I would've never met you."

Theodore wiped a tear off his cheek and let out a rattly breath.

"Yeah," he whispered. He looked back over at me, finally, and met my eyes. "I'm sorry, Jesse."

I could tell he meant it. He didn't apologize unless he really meant it. In fact, I don't think I'd ever heard him apologize for anything before.

"I know." I wasn't sure if I was completely ready to forgive him, but I leaned in and gave him a kiss, anyway.

I scooted over to lean into him on the bed and looked up at the clock on the wall. It was past ten, and it was getting close to time for him to be able to leave the hospital. He had been there for almost six hours, and the nurse who came in to check on him told us they felt comfortable with the diagnostics, and he was as out of the woods as he could be.

She warned him there could be side effects mentally in the months to come and advised him to set up an appointment with a counselor—they could give him a referral. I scoffed, sure there was no way Theodore Townes would ever see a damn therapist. But he nodded and asked her to set him up with a referral, which she did.

I smiled and squeezed his hand. I wasn't sure what was coming. I knew it would probably be a challenge, but I was proud of him. It took a little of the sting off, knowing he wasn't just talking the talk. He was serious about making a change.

"If you want to gather your things, it looks like we're about ready to let you go," the nurse said and left the room.

He squeezed my hand back and gave me a kiss when she walked out.

"I really am sorry," he said. "I'm probably gonna need your help with this whole therapy thing. Can't say I've ever done that before . . ." I saw his tongue fighting with his lips and teeth to find the right words. "This scared me, Jess. I've never been scared like this before. I've had a gun pointed at me. I've stood on great heights. I've driven over a hundred. I've never felt that damn scared—and I'm scared of what's next, too."

"Okay," I said, the only thing I could. "I'll be here every step of the way, Unabomber."

I gave him another kiss, and he stood up to collect his wallet and keys and put on his watch from the table on the other side of the room. His coat was draped over a chair, so I picked it up and handed it to him. He put it on, and I helped adjust the collar then rested my hands on his chest.

"It's going to be okay," I told myself as much as I told him. "Let's get out of here."

"It's almost lunchtime," Theodore said as we made our way down to the lobby.

"I suppose I am pretty hungry." I hadn't realized it with everything going on, but I hadn't even had a cup of coffee all morning, just the glass of ice water Christina had gotten me back at the office, and that had been a while ago. "Where to?"

"Not sure. I feel like I should eat a salad or something."

I chuckled. "Have you eaten a salad in your life?"

"There's a first time for everything." Turns out he still had that damn grin.

Christina was still downstairs waiting for us when we got there. I was surprised. I hadn't expected her to wait for us. I was planning to just get a taxi for us.

"Jesse." She waved us over and stood up when she saw us. She had been reading a newspaper and tucked it under her arm. "And you must be Theodore." She smiled and extended a hand. "It's great to finally meet you—and to see you in one piece," she added.

Theodore took her handshake but also went in for a hug.

"I tell you what"—he turned on the full charm—"I'm mighty glad to be in one piece, too. Theodore Townes, it's a pleasure."

"Christina Klein, I work with Jesse." It was awfully generous of her to frame it that way. More realistically, I worked *for* her.

"Oh, I know who you are," he replied with his own generosity. "Jesse tells me you're goddamn good at your job."

"Does she?" I thought I might have seen her blush. "That's very kind of her. When you work with good people, everything else is easy."

"Ain't that the truth," Theodore replied and bumped me with his arm and a big grin.

"So where are we going?" Christina asked.

"Back to city hall," I said. "I'll get my car and take Theodore from there. Thank you, by the way. You've been way too kind today."

"Oh, it's the least I could do, dear."
"Still."

It felt like the day hadn't warmed a degree when we got out of Christina's car at city hall. It wasn't even cloudy; the air was just frigid. It was one of those days when the sun couldn't even help. The false thaw from the night at the farm had faded thoroughly back into winter—as the weather is wont to do in the mountains. Winter wouldn't be over for another month, no matter what the calendar told us.

"Mayor Wright wanted me to tell you that you don't need to come in tomorrow, but if you do decide to come in to certainly take your time coming in," Christina told me as we parted ways. "There are more important things than getting here early in the morning. You need rest. Take care of yourself, Jesse."

I smiled and thanked her. It was a nice gesture to give me permission to take the day off, but I still intended to go into work. I would have felt guilty if I didn't. Express permission wasn't enough to avoid that. I still felt a responsibility to show up. That was hard to let go.

* * *

"So did you call the mayor's office this morning?" I asked Theodore as the waitress brought us coffees.

"No, actually, I didn't know you were coming until the nurse told me," he said then chuckled. "Nah, I didn't have to call you. You're my emergency contact, Jess! The damn cops called you."

"Wait but that doesn't explain why they called Mayor Wright's office and not my cell?"

Theodore reached into his back pocket and pulled out his wallet. From the beat up and fading leather he pulled out a folded piece of paper and handed it to me.

In all caps at the top of the paper it read, *IN CASE OF EMERGENCY*, in Theodore's scrawled handwriting.

Underneath that he had written simply: *Jesse who works for the Mayor.*

I smiled then laughed and looked back up at him. He was grinning at me with a proud look in his eyes.

"Not sure that's the best strategy there, Teddy." I poked and handed him the paper back.

"Worked, didn't it?"

"I can't argue with that," I conceded. "I'm glad it did. I thought I'd lost you when Mayor Wright started talking."

"Yeah." He looked down into his coffee, and I could see him evaluate his reflection. "Well, I think that's sort of why I wanted them to call his office and not you. I didn't want you to get that call. I especially didn't want you to get that call alone. God forbid I wasn't the one to make it. I can't imagine."

He paused and looked like the emotions would overcome him again. His inimitable spirit had been damaged by guilt and shame, and he was struggling to hide it. I felt bad for him—even more than I felt sorry for myself.

"Yeah." I allowed him a space in the conversation.

"I just can't help but think that you don't deserve that after all you've been through." He looked up at me and took my hand. "I mean, your folks and Katie and all.

It's just too much shit for one person to carry. I don't know if I could live with being one more goddamn burden for you to bear."

"Well, if you were dead, I don't think you'd be living with it, anyway." I tried humor.

"Ha, fair. But I mean now, too. I feel bad," he said. "I wouldn't blame you if you wanted to leave me."

"Oh, shut up, Unabomber." I squeezed his hand. "I love you. Just like I loved Mom, just like I loved Katie . . . hell, even like I loved my father. I'm not going anywhere—you're stuck with me now."

"Is that so?"

"Yeah."

"Goddamn. Guess I really am the luckiest son of a bitch around today."

Twenty-Five

Theodore and I stayed at my place that night. I thought staying at his place might be too isolating too soon for him, and he agreed. I worried about how he would do while I was at work. I worried he would do something he would regret, that he might harm himself in some way.

He assured me he was okay at my place. He promised he would call me if he felt off at all. I did make him agree to call me every few hours or so to check in. Maybe that wasn't strictly necessary, but he'd scared me—and the nurse had scared both of us—and I wanted to make sure he was okay as best as I could.

He called me not fifteen minutes into my workday.

"Jesse," he said urgently.

"Theodore, are you okay?" I grabbed the edge of my desk, and my heart rate went through the roof. It was barely 9:30 a.m., and he had just been sitting on the couch drinking coffee and watching TV when I left. I was terrified what tragedy could have befallen him in half an hour.

"Of course I'm okay!" he exclaimed. I could hear his stupid grin through the phone. "I just got bored and wanted to bug you." He laughed.

I chuckled nervously and shook my head, taking a few deep breaths to try to get my heart rate to come back down.

"Good lord, Unabomber, don't scare me like that."

"All apologies m'dear," he said. "Anyway, I'll talk to you soon. I love you."

"I love you, too." I hung up the phone and smiled into the empty room. He was still inevitably himself. After that call I felt more assured he would be okay. If his first instinct to boredom was to reach for the phone and not drugs, then I would happily take that call every time he rang, no matter how busy I thought I was.

* * *

"Jesse! In already!" I hadn't noticed Mayor Wright open the door behind me. I had just gotten off the phone with Theodore who was calling to mess with me as he started his day—it had become something of a tradition in the few months since his overdose. I turned around, and Mayor Wright looked tired, like he hadn't slept the night before, but determined. "Glad to see you smile. Got time to come talk?"

"Yes, sir." I kept my smile and walked back to his office with him.

We sat down on leather chairs across from each other by a thick glass coffee table.

"Coffee?"

257

"No thanks, I've had too much already." I laughed a little, feeling the heavy thump of my amped up heartbeat. More caffeine was not what I needed.

"Okay." He settled into his seat with a mug full of coffee for himself and took a long sip. He used his bottom lip to extricate the residual coffee from his bearded top lip.

Mayor Wright picked up a couple of papers from the table, leaned back, and folded his legs. His pants pulled up to reveal his cowboy boots, well-worn from years of prior hard labor before becoming mayor.

"First of all, how is Theodore?" He met my gaze with genuine care and concern.

"He's good. He actually just called me to check in and give me a hard time," I said. "He's going to be just fine, already back to his old self, cracking jokes. He finally quit his job bartending. The late nights weren't so good for his mental health, and he's even started seeing a counselor, which I wasn't expecting him to do, so I'm glad of that. I just hope he keeps following through, and I really hope he stays clean."

"Yeah." Mayor Wright looked down a little. "Yeah, well, that's the hard part, isn't it? It's hard to make that big a change. If I can be of any help—personally or with this office—I'll do what I can do to make his life easier. You both deserve it."

"I appreciate that, sir."

He shuffled the papers he was holding and handed me a pack of stapled pages.

"I took the liberty of drawing up a memo," he said. "It has already gone to the city council and later today, with your blessing, Christina is going to send it to the governor and the party leaders in each chamber of the general assembly.

"It is, as you'll see, a summary of the first three months—the first quarter—of your overdose mitigation program," he continued. "It has gone through analysis by the folks at the hospital, by the Bellwether Police, and compiled by Christina. The news was a surprise to me, and I think may even shock you. It turns out, according to our data, that Theodore was not the only person saved by this program.

"In all, nine doses of naloxone were used over three months in seven separate instances. In all seven cases the drug was administered on time, and the person suffering the overdose made a full recovery. That's seven lives saved, Miss Jesse."

"Wow," I whispered, mostly to myself.

"The better news," he continued. "Is that this is without us putting out any sort of marketing campaign. We didn't advertise the program, no flyers, no interviews in the newspaper, nothing. So a lot of folks probably didn't even know about it—but the folks who did, or who happened to be in the right place at the right time, were able to make use of it.

"I wanted to tell you this to tell you that this is a great thing—a damn great thing—and I was wrong to be hesitant about it. You made this happen, and a lot of folks owe you their thanks."

"I appreciate that, sir." I swallowed the lump in my throat as I was welling up.

"Now there's the other news. Thanks to what Theodore told the police, they were finally able to make an arrest. Not to simply take drugs off the streets, but to take unclean drugs off the streets," he said, emphasizing his point with his hands.

Jack, I mouthed. I was shocked, and relieved, that he finally got caught. I never thought I'd see the day.

"This is a good start and all, but it's made me do a lot of thinking. I want to push for more, and I want you to help me." He uncrossed his legs and leaned in toward me. "You're smarter than you lead on, Jesse—and you're certainly smarter than you think. I want to promote you to being a policy advisor to me. It's not a huge raise, but it's a significant change in your role and one I think you're ready for.

"For goodness' sake, Jesse, you don't need to be answering the phone and typing in spreadsheets for the rest of your life. You deserve better than that. Plus, Bill told me you're going to need a little more work to keep you busy now that he's retired." He winked.

I was shocked and taken aback by the offer—and I must admit, a little bit proud.

"You don't have to answer now, but the first thing I want to work on is designing a pilot program for bolstering harm reduction." He kept going. "I think that I'm ready to consider a supervised consumption program to help folks who are addicted to opioids make progress safely, so we don't lose more folks who might otherwise seek help.

"Of course, I'm still not 100 percent sold on the whole thing, but that's because you haven't finished convincing me. So that's why I need you advising me and helping me out. But from what everyone has told me, this might be a good step in the right direction, even if it hurts my re-election chances. But I think I'm still pretty safe in that regard." He grinned at me in a way I hadn't seen from him before.

He knew he was good at his job, and he knew there was no one else in Bellwether who could do it better. I admired that confidence, and I admired his humility in changing his mind. From where he was just a year before to that day was remarkable, and I was prouder to work for him than I'd ever been before.

Twenty-Six

Life with Theodore had been odd since his overdose. We hadn't talked about our situation at all, really. I think I mostly didn't want to upset the order of things. I wanted to keep it safe, keep *him* safe. I also knew I still wanted to be with him—Christina's talk had thawed me.

We had also taken up a new hobby: walks after work. An attempt to help him gain strength back and a way for me to feel closer to him—and safer with him.

I told Theodore about my day as we walked. My cold and dry fingers intertwined in his, hunting for a little warmth. He pulled me into his body and kissed me on the forehead. His lips were warm on my numbing face.

"So short story long, Mayor Wright offered me a promotion. He wants me to step into a new role as a policy advisor," I said.

"Holy goddamn shit, Jess!" Theodore just about jumped in the air with excitement. "That's fantastic! Are you taking it?"

"Yeah, I think so."

"Wow, I'm really proud of you."

"You're dating a professional politician now, Unabomber." I looked up at him. He seemed taller than I remembered. I loved how I felt standing beside him. Safe. "Got to shape up."

"About that," he said and slowed down his gait. I felt a pit in my stomach. "I've been doing a lot of thinking on account of my recovery and not working at that damn bar anymore. Anyway, I didn't think there would be anything left for me after my divorce—and falling in love with you certainly wasn't part of the plan. But I guess change is sort of constant in this weird world, and I almost died just a few months ago—that's not lost on me."

"Okay," I said nervously, prepared for the breakup that would surely undo me, even if I still carried some anger toward him. Losing Jeff, a man I didn't love was hard enough—losing someone I did love was sure to be harder.

"So I think that it's time to commit to a better life, you know?" He stopped walking and shoved his hands in his coat pocket. He looked nervous. I don't know that I'd ever seen him look truly nervous just talking. "Anyway, any better life for me is going to have to have you in it and is going to involve a little more commitment from me to doing things the right way, every day."

He got down on one knee and pulled a ring box out of his pocket.

"I also think that doing things that scare me might be good sometimes. So I got off my ass and found a job. It ain't much, just entry level work with the Sanitation Department, but I got to start somewhere, right?

"And I did some shopping—well, that's a lie, I did this shopping a while ago—and in your closet at home you'll find that dress from the mall," he said, welling up, but sure. "Taking the leap again after how it ended last time terrifies me, but you ain't Mary, and I ain't Jeff.

"Jesse, will you marry me?"

* * *

After my divorce from Jeff, I was a cynic. I thought marriage was for the blindly hopeful and the stuck in place. I thought nothing could last—certainly not in Bellwether. I thought my folks' marriage was how long-term marriages would end. I thought. I thought. I thought.

I was wrong. Theodore made me feel a way I never had before. He had flaws, but so did we all. He didn't seek out drugs, drugs seek out anyone they can get. The opioid epidemic knows no bounds, no mental fortitude. I'd lost my first best friend to it—I wasn't going to lose my second.

After so much loss, it was time to gain and to change the ending, on my own terms, of my long-enduring Appalachian nightmare. It was time to take a leap, not from something, but *to* something.

"Theodore." I mirrored his grin. "I'll marry the hell out of you . . . Yes."

Acknowledgements

Thank you to my friends and family for their support on the journey of writing this book.

Thank you to Danielle Lange for her brilliant editing services helping the book get over the finish line. Your work took the book from a hopeful endeavor to something I could be proud of.

Thank you to Mom, Dad, Shelby and Bodie Craig. Y'all believed in me even when I didn't believe in myself.

Thank you to the lovely Erin Miller. You have been steadfast in your support and ceaselessly by my side.

Thank you to Zach Berly for his continued support of my writing.

Thank you for my Radford friends—Greg, Nate, Sammy, Shelli and so many more who influenced this novel. Though my time in Appalachia has been short so far in my life, what it revealed in my spirit will be with my forever.

Lastly, thank you to my East Carolina colleagues, especially Coach Kim for her remarkable humanity and care for my endeavors.

About the Author

Cole William Barnhill is a born and raised North Carolinian whose year living in the Virginia mountains was formative in his approach to writing. He is a graduate of the University of North Carolina with a dual major in English and Comparative Literature and Political Science. He currently lives in Greenville, N.C. where he works in collegiate athletics communications.

www.ingramcontent.com/pod-product-compliance
Lightning Source LLC
Chambersburg PA
CBHW022030240626
47154CB00007B/2346